Adina turned and r... porch, looking back... charging toward her.

She'd made it to the other side of the long, narrow porch, where the second set of steps would take her away from the man, her heart pounding with fear, when someone reached out and tugged her around the corner. Adina stiffened and tried to pull away.

"Shh." He held her in front of him, his hands on her arms.

Nathan.

Adina let out a long breath. "You scared me."

"Not any more than that stranger who just broke in," he whispered in a harsh tone. "Did he get away?"

She guided him toward the steps to the small back courtyard. "I managed to break loose but he's still here." She pointed to the other side of the porch. "He'll find us if we don't do something."

Nathan flipped her around, his eyes wild with concern and fear. "You go down and into the kitchen. I left the door open in my haste. Stay put, Adina. Do not go anywhere. You wanted my help, well, now you've got it."

With over seventy books published and millions in print, **Lenora Worth** writes award-winning romance and romantic suspense. Three of her books finaled in the ACFW Carol Awards, and her Love Inspired Suspense novel *Body of Evidence* became a *New York Times* bestseller. Her novella in *Mistletoe Kisses* made her a *USA TODAY* bestselling author. Lenora goes on adventures with her retired husband, Don, and enjoys reading, baking and shopping...especially shoe shopping.

Books by Lenora Worth

Love Inspired Suspense

Undercover Memories
Amish Christmas Hideaway
Amish Country Secret
Retribution at the Ranch
Disappearance in Pinecraft

Rocky Mountain K-9 Unit

Christmas K-9 Unit Heroes
"Hidden Christmas Danger"

Alaska K-9 Unit

Christmas K-9 Protectors
"Alaskan Christmas Chase"

Visit the Author Profile page at LoveInspired.com for more titles.

Disappearance in Pinecraft

LENORA WORTH

LOVE INSPIRED SUSPENSE
INSPIRATIONAL ROMANCE

LOVE INSPIRED® SUSPENSE
INSPIRATIONAL ROMANCE

ISBN-13: 978-1-335-59806-6

Disappearance in Pinecraft

Recycling programs
for this product may
not exist in your area.

For questions and comments about the quality of this book, please contact us
at CustomerService@Harlequin.com.

® is a trademark of Harlequin Enterprises ULC.

Love Inspired
22 Adelaide St. West, 41st Floor
Toronto, Ontario M5H 4E3, Canada
www.LoveInspired.com

Printed in Lithuania

MIX
Paper | Supporting
responsible forestry
FSC® C021394

Before they call, I will answer;
and while they are yet speaking, I will hear.
—*Isaiah* 65:24

In memory of my sister, Gloria Palmer.

ONE

Someone was following her.

Adina Maas turned and saw the vehicle headed through the moonless night directly toward her, its lights so big and bright she held up a hand to shield her face.

Then she panicked, a deep fear racing through her mind, her hands clutching her backpack, its weight like a shield on her shoulders. She hurried away from the bus station in Sarasota, Florida. The Pinecraft Mennonite Tourist Church looked safe enough after she got off the bus and mingled with the crowd. But the other passengers greeted friends or family and went on their way, leaving Adina to wait.

No one had come to pick her up. Where was her sister, Blythe? She'd promised she'd be here. Surely the big vehicle creeping in a spidery way behind her wasn't Adina's ride to Blythe's home. Blythe had told her not to take a ride from anyone else.

She turned. The truck still hovered nearby, its heavy motor purring like a lion about to pounce. But Blythe wasn't in the truck. Just a man staring at Adina.

Even though she had the address, she had no idea where to start in finding her sister's winter home. Confused, she kept walking and tried to join a crowd of Amish to blend in and ask for directions.

Did someone know she'd slipped away from Campton Creek, Pennsylvania? She had to find out why her sister wasn't answering her letters or the messages she'd left when she visited the phone booth. Adina thought about the last message she'd gotten from Blythe: "*Kumm* to Pinecraft by bus. I'll buy your ticket and be there to pick you up when you arrive at the church drop-off. Do not accept a ride from anyone else. Please *kumm*, sister."

After Adina had confirmed the one-way ticket Blythe had booked, she'd gathered her meager earnings, then sneaked away from her *aenti*'s house in the middle of the night. Now she was alone in a strange place that was nothing like her home in Pennsylvania.

A town within a city, Blythe had called it. An Amish community unique from any other because it had become a resort of sorts over the decades. Amish vacationed here and some moved here. Blythe had told Adina she and her new husband would be back and forth between Pinecraft and Campton Creek.

You can spend a season with us once we're established and I've learned how to manage two homes. I might need your help.

Now it seemed Blythe did need her help. Fear tickled at Adina's neck. What if someone wanted to stop her from finding her sister? Or just stop her from getting away? Aenti said Adina shouldn't read the romantic suspense novels from the library because they were making her imagine things, but what else did she have to occupy her time? And why didn't Aenti Rita worry about Blythe the way Adina did?

You're just lonely and maybe a little envious, don't you think? Her *aenti* Rita had always accused her of being jealous of her older, more vivacious sister. So now her *aenti* was trying to marry her off in much the same way she'd convinced Blythe to marry.

She thought of Elman Barr, the man Aenti Rita wanted her to marry. A vile, hateful older man who'd told Adina exactly how things would be once they became man and wife. Her *aenti* had plans for both of them to move from their modest house to his big roomy one—with his mother, who was a tyrant like him.

Neh. Adina had taken a lot of flak from her resentful *aenti* since her parents had died after a horrible buggy accident where the *Englisch* driver had been drunk.

While she appreciated her *aenti*'s help, she would not become a maid expected to take care of three capable people who only complained about everything. Adina believed in being kind and considerate, but she did not want to have a loveless marriage with a man who appalled her. She had to find Blythe and see if she could stay with her for a while. Only, Blythe wasn't here to get her. Something was wrong. She and her sister had always been close, but since Blythe had moved to Pinecraft for the winter, her letters had been few and far between. Blythe had sent her the one message and Adina left a message with her arrival time, hoping Blythe received it. Maybe she hadn't.

Searching for a store or restaurant so she could sit down and find Blythe's address in her notebook, Adina checked behind her again.

The big truck hovered behind her, its shadow cast out in a giant slant along the street. Then she heard the vehicle's door slamming.

A heavyset man wearing a black shirt and dark jeans stalked toward her. When he got close, she noticed a strange tattoo on his right arm. Some sort of creepy creature. "Hey, are you Adina Maas?"

Adina didn't want to answer. Blythe had told her not to accept a ride from anyone else. She kept walking, her sneakers squeaking on the sidewalk.

"Blythe sent us," the man called.

Adina whirled and stared at the man. "You know Blythe?"

The man nodded. "Sure. She told us to come and get you."

A shiver of warning crawled down her spine. "But I don't know you."

The man leaned over and opened the passenger-side door. "You can get to know me, once you get in. C'mon now."

"*Neh*. I'll wait to hear from my sister."

The man let out a curse word and lifted a gun from his lap. "I said, get in."

Adina took off running through palm trees and huge blossoming shrubs, the coolness of the February night making her shiver, the trees damp with the remnants of an earlier rain. Her heart pounded as her feet hit rough concrete and chunks of tree roots. She turned on another street, hoping the man hadn't followed her. A sleeve caught on budding brambles that slapped against her face in the same way her *aenti* had slapped her time and again.

Then she heard footsteps approaching, the roar of a motor following. She ran behind a cropping of palm trees that lifted out like a dense mushroom, giving her time to catch her breath. The man wasn't going to give up. This wasn't a ride come to take her to Blythe. She knew danger when she saw it.

But she wouldn't give in either. Not this time. She'd given up on getting justice for her parents. The man who'd killed them had money and ruthless lawyers. While Adina and her sister had neither.

Her fears were not without merit after all and there was

no one to tell her she was overreacting or imagining things. So she followed her own instincts and tried to get away. Even though the night was dark and the tropical breeze Blythe had talked about felt balmy against her damp skin, her eyes adjusted enough to find a path that would lead to another lane across the way.

She'd made it across to the other path and breathed a sigh of relief until she heard footsteps behind her. They were still tracking her!

Adina grabbed for the nearest tall tree. She had to hide but she needed to find a building or home to ask for help. She stayed off the sidewalk, moving through fragrant bushes and swaying palm leaves. Soon she came out on the other side and saw another car approaching. She knelt by some bushes and let the car pass before she got back on the road and hurried away, her prayers centered on getting to a safe place.

When she spotted what looked like a café up ahead, she came back to the sidewalk, glad for the streetlights that shined a creamy yellow in the dark. But just as she rounded the corner toward the café, a burly arm reached out and grabbed her.

She tried to scream, but the man with the tattoo put his hand over her mouth and held her close, his breath burning against her skin. "You're just like your sister, ain't you? She never listened either. But you sure will."

Adina's heart raced, her eyes watered, her throat burned. She pushed at him, grunting and trying to scream for help, her feet kicking at his thick jeans, stomping on his leather boots. He laughed and held her so tightly, she thought she might faint. Weak from her long trip, and shocked, she became too tired to fight him off. Useless.

She was being kidnapped and no one in the world knew

she was even here. Adina screamed a silent prayer for help
and asked *Gott* to provide her a way out. But the man tugging her closer and closer to that open truck door didn't care
about her prayers.

Nathan Kohr did a double take and listened again. He'd
heard a strange sound.

A grunt, a yelp like a kitten scooting under a wire. He
glanced back behind him and caught sight of a big man
dragging an Amish woman into the oleander bushes across
the street.

At first Nathan couldn't move. But with a burst of adrenaline, he took off running across the deserted street and into
the trees. Listening, he watched the sidewalk to see if anyone
showed up. Had he only imagined seeing that woman kicking and groaning?

Another sound, like a scuffle, then a male grunting. "That
was a big mistake."

A scream, this time a woman's high-pitched cry.

Nathan followed the echoes over to another block where
he heard a motor roaring. Then someone called out, "Hurry,
the boss is mad enough already."

Nathan pushed through lush green elephant ear plants
and thick patches of six-foot-tall banana trees to come rushing out in a yard three blocks from his mother's quilt shop.
"Hey, what's going on?"

A gunshot rang out. The woman screamed again as Nathan ducked for cover.

"Get outta here, mister." The man holding her glanced
around. "Don't make us have to hurt you or her."

Another man ran up to them, a gun in his hand. "We need
to get her to be quiet and get in the truck."

"*Neh*," the woman who was dressed Amish cried out. "I'm not going with you. I won't. Where is Blythe?"

Blythe? Nathan knew only one woman named Blythe and she was married to a very powerful man. He glanced around, searching for a weapon. Being Amish, he didn't like trouble but he couldn't let an innocent woman be kidnapped right here on the street. Especially an Amish woman.

He spotted some rocks lining a flower bed and hurried to lift several up. The rocks were edgy and jagged, about the size of a softball. He might be able to get in a good throw. The men were dragging the woman, forcing her toward the truck idling down the way.

She kicked and cried out until the one holding the gun slapped her. Then she only sobbed quietly as Nathan worked to get one of the rocks in his throwing hand.

Without thinking, he ran forward and called out, causing both men to whirl around. One was still holding the woman around her stomach, his hand bleeding. "Hey, wanna pick on somebody? How about me?"

Before they could respond, he took aim and hurled the rock toward the man holding the gun, praying it would hit the mark.

It did. With a grunt, the man let go of the gun after the rock slammed into his shoulder. Nathan rushed toward the man holding the crying woman, growling like a tiger about to attack. Then he aimed the smaller rock at the man's head.

And whacked him on his temple.

Caught off guard, the man let go of the girl and screamed in pain.

Nathan kept going until he'd tackled that one and slammed him against the one moaning on the ground. Standing up, he grabbed the woman. "*Kumm*," he said, out of breath. "Run."

They took off together, her tiny hand in his as sirens stirred the night. Someone had called in the gunshot.

When they'd made it around several tall, slender evergreen bushes, Nathan finally pulled her to a stop and held her close.

"Are you all right?"

The woman bobbed her head and glanced down at the blood on her apron. "I think so. *Denke*."

Nathan held her there while he checked the area. They heard the truck roar to life but a police car spotted it and took off after it, the sound of sirens and the big motor echoing off in the distance.

"You're safe now," he said, finally taking the time to look into her eyes. When he did, he let out a breath. She looked just like Blythe Meissner. And if she was Blythe's sister, Adina, Nathan wanted no part of what she might be caught up in.

"Hey," he said, holding her, feeling her pulse bumping against her wrist. "Why were those men after you?"

She looked down and then back at the street, as if to make sure her attackers were really gone. "I don't know. They were trying to force me, but I slammed my backpack into the nose of the one who grabbed me. A piece of the broken buckle jabbed him and he started bleeding. He wiped at it and then grabbed me again."

That explained the scream earlier and the drops of blood on her clothes. "That was brave."

"Not really. I was terrified."

The woman looked up again and into his eyes. Nathan drew back, his gaze moving over her face. Recognition colored his world and brought back memories.

"Adina?" he asked, remembering her eyes were so very different from Blythe's. Blythe had dark eyes, almost onyx. Adina's eyes were a sweet, deep blue, like the deepest depth of the ocean. "Adina, it is you," he said again. "What are you doing here?"

Adina took in breaths of air then turned to look at the now empty sidewalk. "Nathan, I'd forgotten you moved to Pinecraft but I'm so thankful you're here. I really need your help."

Nathan stared at her with such an intense gaze, Adina wanted to turn and run away. He'd never forgiven her sister for breaking his heart during their *Rumspringa* years ago back home. But she couldn't run anywhere now. She gave Nathan a once-over, too, taking in his stormy gray eyes and his shaggy dark hair. He was still sturdy and muscular from hard work. Still handsome. She tried to forget what a big crush she'd had on him years ago. Those days were over, so she sent her memories scurrying for cover.

"I'm sorry," she said, getting right to the point even if her voice was shaky, "I came here to visit Blythe. But I think she's in trouble and I have nowhere else to turn. I have no idea why those men tried to take me." She shivered and shook her head. "Something's not right but I intend to find my sister. I came here for so many reasons, all of them wrong. But now that I'm here, I'm not going back home until I find Blythe."

TWO

Nathan let her fierce declaration soak in. It'd been years since he'd seen Adina. She'd been a young girl when he left Pennsylvania, but now she was definitely a grown woman.

"Did you come all the way from Campton Creek?"

She nodded, her cheek bruised from being slapped. "I wanted to stay with my sister for a while. But she wasn't at the bus station, so I started walking. Those men followed me and tried to take me with them. I honestly don't know what's going on."

Nathan sympathized with her despite his misgivings regarding her sister, so he tried to offer her reassurance.

"Let's get you inside and out of this damp weather. My *mamm* and I live a few blocks from here. I was on my way home when I heard a commotion and saw a man dragging you away."

"I don't know who he is," she said again. "He followed me from the bus station and told me he'd take me to Blythe. I didn't even know there was another man with him. He must have been in the smaller bucket seat in the back."

Nathan's expression turned ominous, his dark eyebrows shooting up. "You came here to visit and Blythe didn't show up to get you?"

She shook her head. "I sent her a message about my arrival, but I don't think she saw it. It's not like her to ignore me." Wiping at her eyes, she said, "I know she didn't send those men to get me, because her one message said not to leave with anyone else. But they did mention her name, so maybe they know where she is. Maybe I should have gone with them just to find her but they were armed. I saw a gun."

"I think you made the right decision," he said. "You'd have been in a world of trouble, here alone and going off with two strange men."

"They scared me when they said I was just like my sister, and that she'd never listened either. They said it in past tense."

"I heard that," he admitted. "There is a lot about Blythe you need to know, Adina." Better to be honest with her up front. She'd walked into a dangerous situation.

The Maas sisters weren't twins. Blythe was two years older than Adina. Nathan had known them back in Campton Creek, but he'd had a bad experience with Blythe. She liked to tease boys and then leave them for the next person. She'd broken up with Nathan years ago when they were young. When he'd heard she'd finally settled on Hayden Meissner, a man ten years older than Blythe who'd inherited his father's propane business, Nathan knew she was in for trouble. The Meissners, who lived in a community near Campton Creek, wielded a lot of power in both Pennsylvania and Pinecraft. Nathan hadn't known them well back in the day and he'd managed to avoid them here for years. But when Blythe came to visit him and his *mamm* here in Pinecraft, it had been hard to ignore how frail she looked—sick almost. Come to think of it, he hadn't seen her in weeks. Now Adina had him really concerned.

"C'mon," he told Adina. She was innocent in all of this. He'd take her home and let Mamm get her cleaned up. "You can stay with us tonight. We have a full apartment over Mamm's quilt shop. Maybe tomorrow, we can see about finding Blythe."

"I know how you feel about her," Adina said, still sounding scared. "She was happy when they left a few months ago to spend the winter down here. Now I just don't know."

"We'll figure things out," he said. "Do you need to let anyone back home know you made it here?"

"*Neh*," she said too quickly. "You see, I wasn't just coming here to find Blythe. I need to get away from an arranged marriage. I doubt I can ever return home again."

Nathan let out a sigh. "Seems we have a lot to talk about, ain't so?"

"A whole lot," Adina replied. "I'm not the same shy girl you remember from five years ago, Nathan. And after tonight, I don't think I'll ever be the same again."

Flustered that Nathan had been the one to save her, and worried about her sister, Adina found her courage as they entered the door of the Kohr Quilting and Sewing Shop. The two-story building was quaint, all white with black shutters on the windows, and a nice wraparound porch on the second floor. Plain in a way, but also welcoming with colorful fragrant flowers blooming in hanging pots, lush dish gardens and lovely glass French doors that begged to be opened. Two big bay windows on each side of the doors displayed several beautiful quilts in all colors and sizes.

Adina took it all in, her hands still shaking when the jingle of tiny bells announced their arrival. Nathan guided her ahead of him, carefully watching the street. Four Amish women glanced up from their stitching to stare at Adina with rapt curiosity.

One woman gasped and then stood, her expression full

of surprise and interest. "Blythe?" Then the woman looked again. "Adina Maas, what on earth are you doing here?"

Adina realized she'd been mistaken for her sister. Maybe she had held a bit of resentment. Would she always be in Blythe's shadow?

"*Ja*, it's me, Ruth," she managed to squeak out. "Adina."

Ruth rushed across the room so fast, her apron made a swoosh. "Let me have a look at you? What happened to your face?" With a gasp, Ruth saw the blood on her apron. "Oh, my. Nathan, what has happened?"

Nathan hesitated and then said, "Adina was mugged after leaving the bus station. Two men tried to take her backpack when she was walking from the bus drop-off and she fought one of them. That's his blood on her apron."

"Oh, my." His mother and her friends gave Adina a once-over, all of them sighing and shaking their heads. "I'll get you a clean apron in a minute. But first, are you sure you're okay?" Ruth held Adina's chin with a gentle hand.

Adina blinked back tears. "I am now."

Nathan had covered for her and probably for Blythe. The men were after her, not her precious backpack. It had been a Christmas gift from Blythe. The colorful butterfly motif reminded her of her spirited sister. Adina carried it everywhere, which had only annoyed her *aenti*.

Now Ruth looked at her with so much sympathy and kindness, she wanted to sit and have a *gut* cry. She'd missed her *mamm*'s friends. Aenti didn't have many friends and she'd run off the ones who'd tried to reach out.

"Should we report this?" Ruth asked Nathan.

"Someone called the police because one of the men shot at us," Nathan said. "I thought it best to get Adina away from there. But I will let them know and give them a de-

scription of the truck. A patrol car did come and it was following the truck as it sped away."

"Shot at you? I hope they catch them," Ruth said. "We
rarely have things like that happening around here."

"I didn't expect that either," Adina said in a weak voice.

"What in the world brings you to Florida?" Ruth said,
after ushering her in and telling Nathan to lock the door.
"Let me get you some lemonade, and a warm rag for that
nasty knot on your face."

The three other women kept their gazes glued to Adina.
Finally, Ruth noticed and shook her head. "I'm sorry. I was
so shocked, I forgot to introduce you. Ladies, this is Adina
Maas, one of my best friend's daughters. Nan was such a
sweet woman. Adina and her sister, Blythe, who you've
all met, lost their parents a few years ago in a buggy accident. I lost a *gut* friend in their mother. Adina lives with her
mother's sister, Rita. Although, unless she's changed, Adina
has probably had enough." Then she put her hand over her
mouth. "I'm so sorry."

Adina smiled despite the pain of losing her parents,
thinking Ruth had nailed her *aenti*. Not the easygoing
type, that one. Deciding to be honest about that, if nothing else, she said, "I did leave to take a break. I'm here to
visit Blythe, but she didn't show up to get me. So I started
walking, hoping to find a business I could enter and use
the phone or at least check her address again."

"Well, that's odd, but maybe you just missed each other.
But I'm so glad Nathan was able to help you."

She sent her son what looked like a worried glance, and
then went on. "Adina, this is Betty, Diane and Ellen. They
are some of the best quilters I've ever known. We quilt late
once a week and tonight was our night." She motioned to
Adina. "*Kumm* and I'll show you the washroom. Then you

can sit here while I get supper. We live here, mostly up-stairs, but the kitchen and Nate's room and office are down here, behind the shop."

Adina found the dainty little powder room and gasped when she saw her face. She removed the bloodstained apron and folded it over. Taking the warm, wet cloth Nathan had brought to her, she touched the painful bruise on her right cheek. Not the *welkom* she had expected. She could have been killed tonight.

What if Blythe had been harmed or worse?

Adina calmed herself. She couldn't help Blythe if she was falling apart on arrival. She hurried back out to the storefront and placed her apron by her backpack then tried to take in the beautiful materials folded on the shelves and the amazing quilts lining the walls.

The women all nodded and smiled, but remained curi-ous, their eyes gleaming with questions. Adina guessed they had a lot to say about Blythe and her waywardness. Her sister was a "free spirit," as the *Englisch* said. She fluttered around like a butterfly and had only settled on Hayden Meissner because Aenti pushed her and reminded Blythe that he had money and power.

Two things her sister had always craved.

Now here Adina sat, wondering what to do next.

"Your work is lovely," she finally said, admiring the starburst panels on the pastel quilt they had on the table. Maybe if she talked about something else, her nerves would settle down.

That got all of them talking, thankfully.

"*Kumm*," Ruth said after she'd made her way back from the kitchen. She carried a tray of hot tea, sandwiches and cookies. "I always prepare a light supper on quilting days. I'm sure you're still a bit unsteady after being assaulted, so we'll sit here with you while you rest and try to eat something."

Adina took a sip of tea and nibbled on a cut sandwich of roast beef and cheese, wondering if she was truly welcome here. She tried to make conversation. "I'm really glad to see you and Nathan again. I'm thankful that he brought me here."

Nathan had taken a seat on a bar stool near a quilting table, his sandwich big and full of sliced beef and Swiss cheese. "I was on my way here. The attack happened a few blocks away."

"My son would never let a woman be abused or hurt." Ruth looked serene and sure. "He was in the right place at the right time and I'm thankful for that, too. You're safe here, Adina."

Adina nodded and sipped her tea, hoping her shaking hands wouldn't cause her to splash it over the saucer. "I don't want to bring any danger to you though."

Nathan stood and studied her. "I'm going to alert the police about those men. The Sarasota Police Department is one of the best in the state of Florida. They would surely frown on a woman being assaulted."

"*Denke*," Adina said, wondering if the police could help her find Blythe, too. Then she looked over at her backpack. "We need to give them my apron."

The women all looked confused.

"The man's blood is on there." More confusion.

"DNA," she said. "They can run a test to see if it matches anyone in their database."

"How do you know that?" Ellen asked, her tone full of awe.

"I read a lot of books," she explained. "It's just my *aenti* and me and some nights it's hard to get to sleep."

"I'd reckon so after reading about crime all night," Diane said, grinning. "My daughter, Clara, likes to read a lot. I think she knows Blythe from previous frolics. Maybe she can give you more details about Blythe. I know they liked to meet up at the tea shop just up the street."

"That would be helpful," Adina replied, hope filling her heart. "We could meet there, too, if she'd like."

After Diane wrote down her home address, she said, "If you need anything, *kumm* to see us. Clara could use the company. She'll be glad to know you're here. She's mighty concerned about Blythe."

Adina studied the address and then put the note in her backpack, wondering if she'd be able to meet and talk to Clara soon. "I'll remember that. *Denke.*"

Nathan stood and found a big plastic storage bag. "Even I know we need to preserve the evidence. If you don't mind giving me your apron, I'll put it in here and we'll take it to the police tomorrow."

"Have you been reading crime stories, Nathan?" his *mamm* asked with surprise.

"I listen to the news on the radio sometimes, *ja.*"

"You two can team up to find out what's going on," Betty said. "I'm impressed."

Nathan shrugged. "I'm going to the office to report this. I'll be right back."

Adina watched him go into a small room behind the stairs, her worries steaming away like the tea in her cup. "I wish this hadn't happened."

"So you have no idea where Blythe could be?" Ruth asked, giving her friends a knowing glance. "Maybe she sent you another message and you left before you heard it. You know how those phone booths work. Sometimes, messages don't get through."

"I don't think that happened," Adina replied, careful not

to blurt out her other reasons for coming here. "We were clear on her meeting me once I arrived."

Betty's hazel gaze held her. "You for certain sure look like Blythe."

"You know her?" Adina asked, wondering how much they did know regarding Blythe.

"They've met her here in the shop," Ruth said, lifting her hand to her three friends. "These are my confidantes, Adina. As you know, after my husband Dan's heart attack, we decided to move to a new community." She shook her head. "I was leery at first, but having relatives here helped and this climate suits my arthritis much better." She touched Betty's hand. "These three will keep this between us."

Adina nodded. "I think that's best for now. Blythe loves it here, too. She's often talked about the beauty in Pinecraft. The ocean and bay. I can't wait to see all of it."

"She used to stop by here for quilting fabric," Betty said. "I work here part-time, too. But she hasn't been in lately."

That scared Adina. "I'm concerned about her. Her letters have dwindled down a bit."

"You can call her from the shop phone," Ruth suggested.

Nathan came back a few minutes later. "Nathan, take Adina to the phone."

He walked over to help Adina up. "Are you sure you don't need to see a doctor?"

"I'm okay now," she replied. "What did the police say?"

He ran a hand down his face. "They took the description I gave them and told me to bring the apron in. They'll send it to the state lab, but it might take a while to get any evidence back."

"I really appreciate your help, Nathan. Do you know a good hotel or bed-and-breakfast? I have a little money."

"Don't worry about that," Nathan said. "If I know my *mamm*, she'll have you a bed ready upstairs in no time."

"That's for certain sure," Ruth replied, her smile sincere. "We can't let you go stay with strangers after what happened."

Adina shook her head. "I won't burden you like that. I just need to find Blythe."

"We'll talk about that later," Nathan told her. "Let's try calling her. This might only be a misunderstanding."

She followed him into the office and took the phone he handed her. Hitting the keyboard with the number she'd memorized, she turned to Nathan. "It's ringing." Then she listened as the phone went to a voice message. "Blythe Meissner is not available right now. Please leave a message after the beep."

Adina waited, hoping to make contact. "The message box is full," she told Nathan. Then she hung up the phone. "That's odd because this is her emergency phone. She rarely uses it."

"Some Amish carry phones all the time now," Nathan said. "Especially here where we live in a city, rather than a rural area."

"But to have a full message box. That's not like Blythe. She knew to only use it in emergencies or when she needed to talk to her husband. He travels a lot."

Nathan glanced toward the curious women in the room. "Adina, let's get you where you can rest. I'll go with you to Blythe's house first thing tomorrow. I promise."

Adina was too tired and confused to argue with Nathan. After saying good-night to Ruth's friends, she followed Ruth upstairs to a nice, clean little room with double doors that could be opened to the second-floor porch. She'd stay here tonight, but tomorrow she had to find Blythe. Where could her sister be? What if she'd come here only to find out the worst about Blythe's life? What would she do then?

THREE

Adina woke with a start and sat up. Near dawn. A *gut* time for her to leave quietly. She was used to getting up early but today, just then, something had woken her. Had she heard a noise or was she just dreaming a bad dream?

Remembering where she was, she blinked to clear her sleepy eyes and saw the last of the faint moonbeams floating through the sheers and blinds. But the vista of a sleepy sun shimmering over water off in the distance made her remember how she'd opened the doors out onto the balcony last night. The building was situated in a great spot to catch the sun rising and setting from either corner of the big wraparound porch.

Nathan and Ruth had been kind but having her here could be a danger to them. Nathan had protected her by not mentioning what those men had said about Blythe, and while she appreciated their kindness, Adina wouldn't get them more involved than they already were.

Why did those men try to take her? What had they done to her sister?

She must hurry. Other than her nightgown, she hadn't unpacked the two other dresses she'd brought, so she quickly put back on her travel dress and freshened up in the hallway washroom. She'd been given a beautiful room, and she loved the double doors to the porch. A nice gesture, but when she returned to get her bag, a prickle of apprehension zinged against her spine in an electric sizzle.

Then she heard another noise. Footsteps on the outside stairs. Followed by a shadow creeping across the porch.

Someone was out there.

If you hear or see anything, wake me, Nathan had told her in a firm voice. *My room is downstairs by the back office of the shop, near the kitchen. And by the way, I'm a light sleeper.*

Would he hear someone walking along the porch up above?

She might have just enough time to run downstairs to the back door.

Adina listened, her breath held as a shadow loomed just beyond the lacy sheers and white blinds. Then the doors rattled, the doorknobs jiggling. Panic set in. Had she remembered to lock the doors?

Trying to decide what to do, she listened and hoped someone would hear the intruder.

The rattling increased. Adina moved toward the closed bedroom door, determined to make it downstairs. Before she'd stepped a foot, the doors burst open and a man came running toward her.

Adina screamed and turned toward the second-floor landing so she could run downstairs, but the man caught her and dragged her back toward the open French doors, his big arms bruising her as he lifted her feet off the floor. She didn't have any weapons except her backpack, which she swung at his head. That had worked earlier.

Then she remembered something she'd read in a book about poking an attacker in the eyes. With all her might, she twisted enough to get her fingers pointed toward his face and with a grunt, she jabbed away. Her fingernails hit skin. She clawed his face and then managed to land her index finger in his right eye.

The husky man let out a howl of pain and sputtered profanity, anger in every word.

Without thinking, she kept poking and hitting until the man's grip on her gave way. She saw his tattoo as he lifted his arms. An octopus maybe? The sea creature only scared her more.

The man grunted and yanked at her, but that allowed her time to twist away for just a second. She turned and ran across to the porch, looking back as the man came charging toward her.

She'd made it to the other side of the long narrow porch where the second set of steps would take her away from the man, her heart pounding fear, when someone reached out and yanked her around the corner. Adina stiffened and tried to pull away.

"Shh." He held her in front of him, his hands on her arms. Nathan.

Adina let out a long breath. "You scared me."

"Not any more than that stranger who just broke in," he whispered in a harsh tone. "Did he get away?"

She tugged him toward the steps to the small back courtyard. "I managed to break loose but he's still here." She pointed to the other side of the porch. "He'll find us if we don't do something."

Nathan flipped her around, his eyes wild with concern and fear. "You go down and into the kitchen. I left the door open in my haste. Stay put, Adina. Do not go anywhere. You wanted my help, well, now you've got it."

Relief mixed with fear washed through her. "What are you going to do?"

Nathan glanced around. "I aim to go and get rid of our guest."

"Nathan?"

"Stay," he said, gruff but with pleading eyes. "Stay, Adina. Hurry down to the kitchen."

She saw he had something in one hand. "Should I get help?"

"I don't need help," he replied as he lifted the baseball bat and turned toward the coming footsteps. "You stay out of the way."

Adina didn't believe him. Nathan wasn't a violent man. She ran down the back steps and instead of leaving as she'd planned earlier, she did as he'd said and ran into the kitchen. Then she searched for her own weapon and saw a big wooden spoon in a bright blue ceramic container full of cooking utensils. Grabbing it, she dropped her backpack and hurried back up the inside stairs to the second floor.

Only to hear a rustle and feet shuffling before Nathan shouted, "Get off my property!"

Startled, she rushed into the room where she'd slept, fear and adrenaline driving her. The doors stood open to show Nathan standing out on the porch with his bat. She leaned close to see if he'd knocked out the intruder. But the porch was empty.

"Is he gone?"

Nathan whirled, his bat up. "I told you to stay downstairs."

"I didn't want you to get hurt."

He glanced at the spoon, gave her a twisted frown. "So that is your choice of weapon?"

Adina held tight, her knuckles white against the tan spoon. "I've never had much experience with weapons. I could have made it work."

Shaking his head, Nathan came inside and put a heavy dresser in front of the doors. "I got in one lick and he stumbled and hurried down the stairs. He'll have a shiner. I'll get this repaired, but for now I scared him off with my bat and my shouting. He's not very *gut* at his job. He made more noise than a stomping-mad bull."

"And he looks like one, too," she blurted, her heart full of relief. "He has a big black tattoo on his right arm. I remembered it from when they tried to take me. An octopus—isn't that a creature of the sea?"

"*Ja,*" Nathan said in a grim tone. "Smart of you to notice."

"I won't forget that tattoo." Then she started shivering. "I can't go through that again. I managed to jab him in the eye and I scratched his face."

Another frown. "I can't say I disagree on him looking like a bull. We'll let the police know. We'll call them to come here and we can both give them a fairly good description. We can tell them that was one of the men from last night. I'm hoping they can get fingerprints."

"I want to wash my hands, but I have his skin under my nails. More evidence." Adina fell against a chair. "They want me. I'm afraid they might kill me. I'm so worried about Blythe."

He guided her toward the inside stairs. "*Kumm,* I'm going to call for help and then I'll check the whole place." Then he put a finger to his lips as they moved past Ruth's room on the other side of the upstairs. "Mamm might still be asleep."

Ruth opened the door to her room. "I'm awake. I came out to help but when I didn't see either of you, I decided I'd best hide away. Should I call for help?" She held a broom in her hand. "Is it safe?"

"*Ja,* he's gone," Nathan said, glancing from Adina with

her spoon to his mom with a frail broom. "I'll get some-one official on this."

Ruth put her broom in the corner. "I'll make some *kaffe* if I can stop shaking long enough."

Adina shivered, her nerves frayed and battered, the im-print of that man's hands still fresh on her skin. "I don't know why these people are after me."

Ruth shot Nathan a look that begged for answers. "I'm not sure what you've stepped into, Adina. I'm just glad Na-than was able to get to you."

They all headed downstairs, quiet after such a shock-ing encounter. Nathan took Adina's spoon and put it on the table. Then he hurried into the office and shut the door.

Ruth started the *kaffe* in the big percolator and then pulled out bread to make toast.

"I can help," Adina said, her hands shaking. "But I have possible DNA evidence underneath my fingernails."

Ruth waved her away, her confusion causing her to snap out her reply. "You've been through a lot since arriving here. Just rest there at the table—you and your DNA. When did Amish girls start learning such things?"

Adina glanced at the woman across from her. "When we had to start learning to protect ourselves," she replied.

Ruth's dark eyebrow lifted like butterfly wings. "*Ach, vell*, I suppose that's *schmaert*."

The same thing Nathan had said. Only Adina didn't feel so smart right now.

Nathan came back in as sirens screamed in the distance. "They're on their way. And they're on the lookout for the man we described." He checked the back alley and then checked the shop. "I think we need to be careful about going to Blythe's home. These people could easily follow us there."

Disappointed, Adina finally nodded. "How can *you* be so calm?" she asked. He looked like an ancient avenger while she shook like a leaf trying to fall off a tree. "A man just broke into your house because of me. I'm still afraid and I can't seem to catch my breath."

Nathan returned the bat to its place in the small washroom then turned to face her. "I've dealt with criminals before. They sneak close but rarely succeed in breaking in like this one did. We have cameras installed downstairs to prevent this but they only show the street and the shop. I'm hoping we got a good recording of our intruder on one of them." He got out eggs and bread. "You'll need breakfast after we talk to the police and then maybe we can find Blythe's house."

Thankful for that, she said, "You have some protection here, then." Maybe focusing on his life would help her settle down and decide how to handle this.

"Necessary when running a business in a tourist town. *Englisch* visitors are fascinated with us, but some of them think they can trick us and steal from us. That does not go well." Then he gave her an encouraging glance. "Don't worry, we're still very much Amish. The water and heat are propane and so is the stove. We do have electricity and a phone for our business, and theft is not that heavy in this area. But it can happen anywhere, so we're prepared."

Ruth's gaze fluttered from her son and back to Adina. "We've never had anything like this before. Why do those men want you, Adina? I need the truth."

Adina put her head in her hands. "I don't know. Truly, I don't. I think…my sister is in serious trouble."

She got up and ran to grab her backpack. "I must leave."

Nathan reached for her arm. Wondering if she'd ever be

safe again, Adina saw his frown as he glanced at her old backpack. "You *were* going to leave, ain't so?"

"I can't stay here—and that's the reason—that man knows I'm here. That means they followed us even after you got me away from them. You had to come to my defense again. You shouldn't be in danger, too."

Ruth came to stand with her. "You can't go out there with these horrible people after you, Adina. Please, stay here where we can help. We will be fine. I figured this has to do with Blythe, and I believe they want you because either you look like her, or someone sent them to keep you away from her. Your sister has married a dangerous man. He might pretend to be Amish, but Hayden Meissner is not being true to his faith. He could have forbidden Blythe to meet you at the bus drop-off. That's probably why she wasn't there."

Adina started crying. "Then I should go to her. I should have let them take me. I might be able to help her."

The percolator rattled and bubbled. Nathan let go of her and marched to the stove to turn the *kaffe* down.

Ruth hugged her close and repeated, "You can't go out there alone. You'd be taken immediately and something awful could happen. We will make this work and we will help you. These people are obviously ruthless."

"I wish I knew what has happened with Blythe. I'm sorry."

Ruth patted her arm. "*Neh*—you are *welkom* in this house, always, even so. I'm sorry about these attacks, but yes, they must have something to do with your sister."

"I believe that, too. They want me for a reason, which means they think I know something or have something that they need." She glanced out at the shimmering dawn light, fear still hitting at her nerves. "I have nothing but the clothes on my back and what I could toss in my backpack along with a few hundred dollars I've saved up."

When they heard a car pulling up to the curb, Ruth looked out the window. "The police are here. Adina, are you up to this?"

"I'll be okay," Adina said, taking the tissue Ruth offered her. "I need to tell them what happened."

Nathan nodded as they all forgot about breakfast.

Two officers came in and Nathan told them his version of what happened both last night and this morning.

Then they turned to Adina. One of the officers studied her and then said, "Tell us why you came to Pinecraft. Start at the beginning."

Adina swallowed her fears and tried to be honest. "I'm worried about my sister, Blythe Meissner. She was supposed to meet me at the bus stop. I came to visit her, but also to check up on her."

"Meissner?" The officers shot each other frowns. "Married to Hayden Meissner?"

Adina's heartbeat did a blip. "*Ja*. They got married last fall."

"I'm sorry to tell you this, young lady, but her husband reported her missing three days ago."

Adina dropped back down on her chair. "I'm too late. I came too late."

"It's not too late yet," the officer said. "You gave us descriptions of your attackers and you have a blood sample from one of these men, and as you suggested, we can scrape your fingernails to also find DNA. If these men have anything to do with your attacks or your sister's disappearance, you might be a big help to her after all."

Nathan looked back at Adina. "Okay. You'll stay here with us until we find Blythe. Don't leave this house without me."

Adina glanced out the window again, still in shock. "I won't."

She was too afraid to do anything. What had her sister gotten into this time?

Nathan must have seen her fear. "I won't let anyone hurt you, okay? We'll figure this out together and we'll find her. No matter what."

Adina couldn't move. Blythe was missing and she might have been able to go to her last night.

Or she might be dead right now.

Blythe might already be dead.

What had happened to her sister?

FOUR

After the police left with a full report and what they hoped was DNA from where Adina had scratched the man, Ruth sat her down with a cup of hot tea and a split buttered biscuit and cherry jam. "You need to eat a bite."

Adina had scrubbed her hands clean, washing them over and over. She couldn't get the image of that hulking man out of her mind. What if he tried again? She couldn't sit here helpless forever and she sure didn't want to live in fear.

Nathan came back in. "The shop is clear. Nothing amiss there but the video only catches people out front, coming and going from the shop. No images of the man we saw last night." Glancing at Adina, he said, "I have an idea and I hope both of you will agree."

"Tell us," his mother said in her calm, quiet voice.

"I think Adina should work with you in the shop during the day, as often as possible. She'll blend in there and not many men show up at a quilt shop." He rubbed his hands together. "And if one does, he will stand out on our camera, for certain sure. And we can call for help."

"That's a great idea," Ruth said. "I have part-time help, but having someone with me all day would be a blessing. Adina won't have to be alone and frightened while she tries to figure this out." She gave Adina a sweet smile. "What do you think?"

Adina let out a breath of relief, the tension causing her shoulders to ache dying down a bit. "I'd love working in the quilt shop, for certain sure. Then I won't feel so bad about having to stay here. A way to pay you back."

"*Ach, vell,*" Ruth said. "But I'd give you a small spending money salary. You'll do a full day's work each day."

"*Neh,* that's not necessary," Adina said. "I have some cash and…Blythe paid for my bus ticket."

They all sat silent for a moment.

Ruth finally nodded and rubbed her hands together. "How 'bout this—if you need cash, let me know. I'll put aside a tip jar for you. Would that work?"

"I can accept that," Adina said, relieved that she'd have a place to stay and work to keep her occupied. "But—I still want to look for my sister."

"Only when I'm with you," Nathan said. "Don't go anywhere by yourself."

"I wouldn't know where to start," she said, feeling better now. "*Denke.*"

Nathan studied her for a moment then finished his *kaffe.* "Now that the techs have dusted for fingerprints upstairs, I have to fix those doors in the guest room, so I'll need to run up the street to get some supplies. I promise I'm going to make them stronger and safer this time."

Ruth laughed. "I should hope so. I have prayed that the man who did this will stay away."

"I've prayed, too," Nathan said, eyeing his baseball bat.

Adina blinked back tears. "You have both been so kind to me. I'll get to the bottom of this, somehow. I believe the authorities will help, but I'm still concerned that something bad has happened to Blythe."

"I'm concerned, too," Ruth admitted. "Hayden Meissner can't be trusted. His *daed* was a *gut* man, but Hayden had other ideas for the propane company after Herman died. I fear he's fallen out of grace and is on the wrong path."

"And he might have taken Blythe with him," Nathan added, his eyes on Adina. "But we will do what we can to find her, Adina."

She could only force a weak smile. She got up to clean the kitchen, busywork her only way to process her long bus trip here and then almost getting kidnapped.

"I'll be back," Nathan said. "I'm taking the delivery cart up to the Dawson Department Store. Tanner has some extra lumber he can sell for cheap and I can fix the doors with that. Then I'll get some new locks—stronger ones—to put back on." He went to the door between the kitchen and the storefront. "Be mindful of anyone passing by, or anyone who looks out of place if they come inside." He paced a bit, then asked, "Should you just close for the day, Mamm?"

"I will do no such thing," Ruth replied, her hands on her hips. "It's daylight, Nathan. And closing might entice them to sneak in and damage my shop."

"I suppose you're correct. The authorities are on the lookout, but keep the door locked until you see legitimate customers."

"Okay, we'll be diligent and you should be careful," Ruth cautioned. Then she turned to Adina. "It's about time to open the shop," she said. "Are you sure you're up to this? Or would you like to rest in my room for a while."

Adina shook her head. "*Neh*, I wouldn't get any rest. Safer that you and I stick together. Let me freshen up and make sure my other apron is clean. I'll need to put on a clean dress. I only brought two extras."

Ruth gave her a bright smile. "Ellen has a daughter about

your size and she left some clothes when she got married. When Ellen comes in today, I'll ask her if she has any extra dresses."

Adina relished clean clothes. "That would be considerate." Then she stopped Ruth before they parted. "Why are you and Nathan being so kind to me? After what Blythe did to Nathan, I mean?"

Ruth shook her head and scoffed. "They were young and it wasn't *Gott*'s will for them to be together, Adina. That was long ago. And as for being kind to you, Nan was my friend. Losing her was almost as hard as losing Nathan's *daed*. I'd do anything to help her daughters."

Adina gave Ruth a quick hug. She missed her *mamm* so much, but Ruth made her feel loved and welcome. Why couldn't her own *aenti* do the same? She feared Blythe had taken a dangerous path.

Adina knew the reason for that. They'd both wanted to find love and contentment after losing their parents. And sometimes, that kind of grief took people to places that weren't the best for them.

Adina thanked *Gott* for Nathan and Ruth. They were the kind of family any woman would love to be a part of. But right now, she couldn't focus on that. She had work to do, and a sister to locate.

Nathan got the materials he needed and then discreetly asked around about Blythe. He only mentioned her to people he could trust, most of them business owners who watched out for each other and kept crime to a minimum. He didn't mention the break-in, but this was a small community and people were already asking him why the police had been at the quilt shop this morning.

"Just someone snooping around," he'd explained, glad

people were used to him carrying wood and supplies since he was the unofficial local handyman.

He had told his friend Tanner what was going on. Tanner had married last year and his wife, Eva, was expecting their first child. Tanner had been a widower with a daughter when Eva had arrived in town. Now they were a happy couple as they worked side by side in Dawson's Department Store.

He envied them even while he was glad for them. After his *Rumspringa* years ago, Nathan had given up on finding the right woman. Blythe's image came to mind, but he knew back then Blythe wasn't ready to settle down. Adina on the other hand, was quiet, hardworking and managed to blend into the background while her sister took center stage. Come to think of it, Adina was more his type.

Whoa. Where had that thought come from? Adina had only been here for less than a day and already his mind was hopping around like a big toad on a lily pad. Besides, she'd brought a whole passel of trouble with her. He didn't need trouble.

Nathan and his *mamm* lived a quiet, content life here. She made a profit with her quilting shop, thanks to tourists who loved to buy handmade Amish quilts and were willing to pay a lot for them. And he kept busy with his handiwork, which he enjoyed. His job had started out as a causal way to earn money while he searched for work, and now it had morphed into a full-time handyman and yard service company. Getting to know the neighbors, both Amish and *Englisch*, kept his days occupied and held his loneliness at bay.

Sometimes he missed the farm and the beautiful countryside they'd left behind in Campton Creek. But most days, he loved the warm climate here and he enjoyed helping people keep their homes in working order. He'd taken courses on remodeling and had found a lot of work through Tanner, who did woodwork for some of the fancy hotels and condos along the coast and in Sarasota. That kept Nathan too tired to worry about finding someone to love.

Not that there weren't women enough for him to find a wife around here. But as his *mamm* liked to say, *None of them seem to stick.*

He was the one who couldn't stick. Too set in his ways, according to a few of the women who'd come bringing casseroles.

And maybe he was.

Right now, he was hurrying along on his navy-blue cart, wood and nails and new locks knocking and rocking as he hit potholes along the sidewalk. When he glanced back to check on his merchandise, he noticed a shiny dark truck following him. One that looked a lot like the truck those men had tried to put Adina in last night. Would these people never give up? Couldn't they let up for a day at least?

Nathan didn't glance back again. Instead he turned down a busy tourist street and caught glimpse of the truck reflecting in the glass shop windows. He pulled over at a lemonade stand, pretending to get a drink and winding up getting some lemonade just to make things look real.

The truck hummed by slowly, then revved up and took off. Nathan did a quick glance and noticed the license plate. Then he grabbed a napkin and wrote down the letters and numbers. Tipping the young *Englisch* girl who'd waited on him, he left to head toward home.

Before that truck beat him there.

Adina had always loved pretty materials so working with Ruth was a real treat. Ruth and Betty had gone over every piece of fabric, telling her what worked best for dresses, aprons and coats. What to sell for *bobbeli* clothing and what would make a pretty ribbon trimmed blanket.

"I never knew there were so many different kinds of scissors or sewing machines," she said in awe after Betty had demonstrated how to sew stretchy jersey, which tended to slide away from the machine needles. "I have so much to learn."

"I was the same," Betty admitted. "I knew how to sew, of course. But Ruth makes it an art form."

After Betty had left for the day, Adina went along the walls, noticing everything, including spools of colorful sturdy threads and rolls of materials ranging from tropical patterns to clean primary colors and the pastels that the Amish here loved to use for summer dresses.

Today, she'd mostly listened and learned how to use the cash register. She'd swept up scraps and bits of thread and tossed it all in a large trash can behind the counter. She'd dusted and straightened things, loving each moment while she tried to keep the panic in her mind from taking over.

"Tomorrow, you can learn more about quilting necessities such as seam rippers, tailor scissors, binders and rulers," Ruth told her. "Those things are needed when we make a quilt or sew a dress." Adina's panic for her sister must have shown, but Ruth misunderstood. "Don't look so horrified. You'll get the hang of things."

Adina blinked and changed her focus. "I should already know a lot of this, but Aenti didn't like us to be too fancy or wear new clothes. She always found us things at thrift stores or mud sales."

Ruth let out a shocked gasp. "Oh, dear, I'm sorry I forced used dresses on you."

"*Neh,*" Adina said, going to the box of clothes Ellen had brought over earlier. "These are like brand-new compared to what I've had to wear." She loved the turquoise and mint dresses and pretty crisp aprons. "These are perfect."

"You can enjoy them knowing Ellen took care of them because she made them," Ruth said, empathy in her eyes.

"Made with love?" Adina smiled. "I haven't had a dress made with love since my *mamm* died."

"Then you'll soon find that we're full of love and gratitude around here."

"I like it here," Adina said. "*Denke*." Then she let out a sigh. "If I wasn't so worried about Blythe, I could enjoy this as a holiday."

Ruth gave her an understanding nod. "All the more reason to keep you busy when you aren't involved in trying to find her."

She could learn quickly if given the chance. Aenti never wanted to give her or Blythe any opportunity to do better. She wanted them under her thumb so she could marry them off, and she always implied they'd need to give her a better life because she'd sacrificed to raise them. But Blythe had outwitted their *aenti* by marrying a man who promised to take her away from that house. And Aenti had not been invited. Neither had Adina, for that matter.

Adina could have a *gut* life right here, she decided. Once she found Blythe and tried to help her get back on the right track. But what if she couldn't find her sister?

What then?

Nathan came hurrying through the front door, causing her to put her dreams and concerns aside. He looked so intense, she had to catch her breath.

"Where's the fire?" Ruth asked, glancing behind him.

"I just…needed to make sure you were both all right," he said, his words winded, his frown heavy.

"Did you see someone?" Adina asked, her heart racing.

"The same truck we saw last night," he finally said. "Headed this way."

"We've not had any strangers in today," Ruth said, closing the blinds and locking the door. "But then, these people would be remiss to even consider showing up in the daytime."

"I don't think they care about that right now," Nathan replied.

Adina watched his face and saw the dread and the dare in that frown. He'd protect his mother and their home, and he'd be forced to protect her, too. She had to do something.

"I know we decided to wait, but tomorrow, I'm going to Blythe's house," she announced. "I need to see for myself if she's hiding there, or if something has happened to her."

"Not without me," he said, the frown softening to a protective stance. "You will not do this alone, Adina. Do you understand?"

Adina understood a lot standing there, staring at the boy who had become a man, the boy she'd pined for while she'd been hidden in her sister's big shadow. Nathan had changed, matured, and now was fully comfortable in his own skin. And handsome at that.

The sooner she solved this mystery and got away from here, the better. She wouldn't fall for Nathan. She couldn't. Because she didn't think he was ready to fall for anyone. Especially a woman who was plain and simple and causing him a lot of problems right now.

"I understand," she said. Then she looked beyond him to the glass shop door, her hand going to her throat. "Nathan, the truck is back—across the street. But I don't see a driver inside."

FIVE

Nathan went into action.

"Mamm, go upstairs with Adina. Go to your room and shut the door. Don't open it for anyone but me."

Ruth grabbed Adina. "What are you going to do, son?"

Nathan grabbed his bat. "I'm going for a stroll around my property. Meantime, you alert the police." He dug through his tool bag. "And give them this license plate number. I got it off that truck."

Ruth grabbed the napkin with his handwriting scrawled on it and hurried Adina upstairs. "*Kumm*, let's do as he says."

He waited, seeing the fear and hesitation in Adina's eyes. She didn't want them involved, but they were now. He'd seen the men who'd tried to take her, and he'd gone up against them, something that must have surprised her and them. Usually, he was a calm, abiding man who followed the tenets of his religion. But he'd do what any man had to do to protect his family—and the woman who'd asked for his help.

Nathan would stay out of a fight, but he'd do what had to be done and somehow, without heavy violence.

Now he prayed that he'd be able to protect his property and Mamm and Adina. He hurried out the back door, locked it and walked around the building. The sunset hovered over the horizon as a reminder that darkness would be here soon. He had to make sure no one was about before that sun slid over the ocean.

After checking the alley behind the building and going up the outside stairs then circling the whole porch, he went down the back stairs to check once again.

Whoever had left that truck there was hiding out, biding his time. The truck was a definite threat and invitation, a way to toy with Nathan.

Did they think Amish men didn't have brains?

He'd turned to go back inside when he heard a thump and then a grunt. Running toward the other side of the first-floor porch, he spotted a man holding his hand to his bleeding forehead as he hurried down the street.

Nathan saw a broken clay flowerpot lying on the ground. He glanced up to where his *mamm* and Adina stood staring down. His *mamm* pointed to Adina. "The girl has *gut* aim."

"Only one this time," Adina said. "I hope the other one isn't hiding out around here."

Nathan shook his head and checked the whole area around the property again. The man had left for now.

When they heard a knock at Ruth's door, Adina jumped, her heartbeats tumbling over each other. After they'd talked to Nathan, they'd gone inside and crouched in a large stuffy closet that smelled of lavender and roses to avoid being discovered by any other intruders.

"In case he comes back," Ruth had told her, urging her into the closet. "He'll be plenty mad that you almost knocked him out."

"I wish I had," Adina replied. Then she sneezed.

Ruth made her own potpourri, she explained to Adina in a nervous whisper. "At least it smells pleasant while we hide."

Adina held a boot—she did have a good throwing arm and she'd be prepared for the next round. Ruth held a candleholder that could do damage to someone's head.

"It's me, Mamm," Nathan called. "It's safe."

Ruth opened the closet door and they scrambled out, taking in air and heaving sighs of relief. Adina hurried to let Nathan in. Seeing that he was not harmed, she whirled to help Ruth.

"I'm okay," Nathan said while they both checked him over. "I found no one else, but this intruder could be waiting for full dark before he strikes again." He glanced at Adina. "If he doesn't pass out from a concussion, that is."

When they heard a knock downstairs, Nathan glanced out the window. "The police are here. At least they didn't alert anyone with their sirens. I'll go down and tell them what happened."

Before he'd made one step, they heard voices shouting on the street. Running to Adina's room, they watched from the window as an officer struggled with a big man wearing dark clothes, his head covered with dark streaks.

"Stay here." Nathan hurried downstairs and out the side door leading to the street. "Hey," he called as he sprinted across the street. "Hey, you?"

The man glanced back just long enough for the officer to draw his gun. "Do not move," the officer said. "What are you doing snooping around this property?"

"I wanted to buy something pretty for my girl," the man said with a smug smile while his gaze drifted up the open doors of Adina's bedroom. "Instead, I got accosted with a flowerpot."

Ruth tugged Adina back from where they stood, but Adina was afraid the man had seen them. "Why can't they leave me alone?" she whispered to Ruth, shivers sliding down her spine. "This has to stop."

Ruth held her hand, pressing her fingers against Adina's damp palms. "*Gott*," she said. "*Gott* will abide."

They listened at the open door while the men's voices carried.

The officer turned the man around and put handcuffs on him. "We ran your plates, buddy. Wanted in two states for robbery, assault and threatening innocent people. We have witnesses who can identify you, so I'd say your days of trying to scare people are over. You won't get to act up once you're behind bars. You'd better be glad that flowerpot wasn't heavier."

The man laughed. "I have a very *gut* lawyer. I can sue."

Adina gasped. "He sounds Amish."

"He probably once was Amish," Ruth replied. "All the more horrible. Hayden must be paying him a lot for him to give up his religion and his soul."

Adina watched as the cop put the man into his patrol car and then took Nathan's statement. The officer looked up at the broken door while Nathan explained again about the break-in last night. Adina hoped she wouldn't need to talk to them anymore. She'd told them everything she could about Blythe and when she'd last heard from her.

Ruth watched her face. "Adina, they will do what they can to find Blythe. You know that, ain't so?"

"I'm hoping and praying," she replied. "But I still need to search for her, too."

"Nathan will take you to her house soon," Ruth reminded her. "That is the first step, but I worry about you taking off on your own. Promise you won't do that. If not for me or yourself, at least for Nathan's sake. Because he's doing his best to protect us. And see out there—already one person is being taken away. We're with you on this."

Adina hugged Ruth. "*Denke.* I'll be careful, I promise. I won't let anything happen to Nathan."

Ruth seemed to accept that promise. "Let's go see what's up down there. I'm mighty tired of these interruptions and I'm hungry, too. Maybe we'll go eat at Yoder's for supper tonight."

Adina didn't think she could eat. Bringing danger to their door had become like a yoke around her neck. She thought about home and her *aenti* back there. Probably worried, but only because Adina's leaving would bring shame to her. Now their *aenti* could lament about both of her sister's wayward daughters.

I can never go back.

She followed Ruth down the stairs, her prayers caught like cobwebs in her throat. What had she done? What had she set in motion? These people could harm Aenti Rita.

Now she had to find her sister, because together they could at least have each other. If Blythe was still alive.

Adina glanced up and saw Nathan coming toward them. If Blythe was dead, she'd be all alone.

Forever.

He wouldn't want her around if something happened to his *mamm.*

"One down and many more to go, I'm thinking," Nathan said now, obviously noticing her stress. "Hey, it's okay. He didn't do any damage. He was trying to sneak away when my friend caught him." He shrugged, then let out a long breath. "I hope he has a headache all night."

Adina finally spoke. "But this can't go on. It's not normal to have to guard your house or put new locks on the doors. Or to have to repair doors. I've obviously stumbled into something that is way over my head. I ran away from home because I was worried about Blythe, but I also left because I couldn't face the future and that horrible Elman Barr that Aenti Rita wanted me to marry. I've made a mess of everything."

Nathan glanced from her to his mother. "Adina, I will marry you myself before I let you go back to that disgusting man. Trust me on that."

Ruth's eyebrows shot up and she actually laughed. "Well, I never."

Adina's heartbeat bumped faster for a new reason now. "You don't really mean that, Nathan. That's going a bit too far in protecting me, don't you think?"

Nathan stood back. "I'm not thinking straight," he admitted. "But…it's not a bad idea."

Then he turned and headed back inside, his handsome face flushed with either exhaustion or embarrassment.

Ruth kept smiling. "What a time this has been. Danger aside, Adina, you sure have brought a lot of excitement to this house."

"The wrong kind of excitement. I won't be here for long," Adina said, her ears still ringing with Nathan's declaration. "I can't go back home because of…things. And I'll have to find my own place here or somewhere. If I live to do that."

"You'll live," Ruth said, seemingly in a good mood even though they were under attack. "My son will certainly see to that now."

Adina's confusion mounted to overwhelming. Nathan didn't mean what he'd said. He'd only been angry in the moment. And yet, he'd planted a bit of hope in her mind, and like a seed about to sprout, Adina experienced something changing in her heart. Something powerful and warm and swift.

What if he'd been a tad serious about marrying her after all?

Early the next morning, Nathan sat in the doorway of his tiny bedroom downstairs, watching the dawn lift in shades of light blue and soft pink. Yesterday, he'd managed to get the upstairs doors patched and he'd bought a new security set-up at a local electronic store. When Mamm suggested walking to Yoder's for a burger, he'd done one better.

"I'll have someone deliver our supper," he'd said, using the shop phone to make the call. This was an emergency of sorts, considering he'd barely eaten since breakfast.

His mother went along with it for once. She had a strict rule regarding their use of modern electronics for anything other than business or an emergency. But she was hungry, too. Adina didn't protest.

Now he had to wonder why he'd blurted out a marriage proposal to Adina yesterday. To grab at a woman with that suggestion while she was dealing with finding her sister and staying alive had to have been the worst idea in his head ever.

But it had kept him awake, so there was that. No one would enter this building tonight. After he filed yet another report with the officers who showed up, he had a few ideas on how to get through the night. He'd set up the new alarm system and motion lights to alert them if any intruders tried to enter the property, and he also found some old-fashioned animal traps he'd brought here when they'd moved.

Now he was awake and keeping watch. He jumped up and walked the perimeters each time a leaf twitched.

The good news—the big truck had been hauled away.

The license plate had brought the authorities a lot of information. Surprised that the criminal hadn't used false plates, he'd found out from one of the officers that the used truck had been purchased in Alabama but the new plates told a tale. The dealer identified the man and the truck because it had a distinguishing mark on it. A deer head sticker the original owner had hand-painted on the tailgate. The car dealer also remembered the man had paid cash for the big vehicle. The locals had gotten a hit on it based on the model and that description. Why would someone with as much money as Hayden Meissner let his henchmen drive such obvious vehicles? Probably to show off his power.

Who knew the ways of the wicked?

According to his friends at the station, the man wasn't talking and he gave them the name of a high-powered lawyer. Nathan prayed the man didn't get out on bond. He could easily disappear. Or do more harm.

Because he couldn't sleep, Nathan had taken out a map and managed to narrow down where the Meissner beach home was located. He would take Adina there, but they'd have to make sure no one guarded it and he'd need to check for an alarm system before they went inside. It could be Blythe was there and needed help. She could be there against her will even though Meissner had reported she'd gone missing. Now he was supposedly out looking for her, but Nathan didn't believe that.

They could check this one time to give Adina some comfort.

First, he'd have to call a taxi. Then he and Adina would dress as *Englisch* and disguise themselves. He hated being deceitful, but they were trying to save someone and he hoped to find out the truth, at that.

Nathan had time to pray a lot, asking *Gott* to protect

them and guide them. He tipped his head against the back of a chair. Ruth had suggested Adina should sleep in her room and he'd moved a cot in there so they could be together and safe. Now that daylight was coming, he dozed off. They'd made it through Adina's second night here and for now, they were safe. Maybe she'd forget about his marriage offer.

He wished he could.

He woke to whispers a little later and the smell of ham frying. Glancing at the sunshine outside, Nathan realized he'd overslept his usual six o'clock getting up time. His old watch showed eight fifteen.

Hopping up, he cleaned up in the washroom and walked out into the kitchen to find Adina and his mother busy with buttering toast and cooking eggs.

"Morning," he said, not looking at anyone in particular.

"*Gude Mariye,*" his mother said. "Did you get some sleep?"

"A few winks right after dawn. I should have gotten up sooner," he said, trying to avoid eye contact with either of them. "I'll get a bite and get busy."

"Sit down," Ruth gently ordered. "You needed to rest and so we let you. But we wanted you to have some breakfast before we open the shop."

"About that," he said. "*Mamm,* ask Betty if her husband, Paul, can *kumm* and sit with you this morning while Adina and I ride by Blythe's house."

Adina's head came up. She'd been avoiding eye contact with him, too. "We're going, then?"

"*Ja,* but we will dress *Englisch.* We'll take the back way to my friend Tanner's store and call a cab from there. That way, we will blend in as tourists if we happen upon anyone asking questions. We might just ride by, but if the place looks deserted, I'll go in and check it out while you wait in the vehicle."

"I'll go in with you if you enter the house," Adina replied with a firm tone. "I won't let you do this alone, Nathan, so let's argue about that now and not when we get there."

His *mamm* coughed under her breath. "I agree with Adina. No one alone, ain't so?"

They had him there. "We'll see how things go."

They ate in silence then he stood. "Mamm, get out those old clothes you bought to use as quilt panels. I think we're in need of looking *Englisch*."

Ruth got busy. By the time she had them dressed in jeans and T-shirts, Betty and Paul had arrived. Paul had *The Budget* newspaper and a book on urban gardening to read, and Betty was talkative, her expressive eyes full of questioning glances.

Nathan guided Adina toward the door, noting she wore a scarf over her chestnut-colored braids. She looked cute as an *Englisch* woman. But he liked her being Amish better. Then he reminded himself that he'd made a clumsy, not-well-thought-out proposal to her. It didn't matter how or why he liked her. She'd be out of his life once they found Blythe. If they found Blythe.

It did occur to him—if Blythe were dead, Adina would truly be alone. Would he have the gumption to propose to her again?

Did he really want that? The image of them together worked down from his head to his heart. He'd known her most of his life, so they had that in common. And she was here and available and pretty and smart. She'd be an asset to Mamm in the shop.

He'd think on all of this. Right now, he had to protect

her. If they survived these attacks, they could probably survive a marriage of convenience.

"Let's go," he said on a gruff tone, causing both Adina and his *mamm* to give him a concerned glance.

Once they were on the way along the back alley, she turned to him. "You can relax, you know. I have no intention of holding you to that offer you suggested last night. I don't think I'm ready for marriage. I'd like to stop running for my life first."

He smiled, realizing she could read him like a book. "I'd like that, too. We need to find out about Blythe right now."

"Ja."

Relief drenched him, followed by a heavy disappointment. His hands got sweaty and his heart hummed. "We can be friends, though, right?"

"I'd like that," she replied. "Just don't get yourself hurt or worse on my behalf, Nathan. I'd never forgive myself if anything happened to you."

"Same here," he replied, his heart thankful for this brief reprieve. Because they did not know what might be ahead.

SIX

They waited on the side street for a taxi. Adina took in the scenery since this was the first time she'd ventured out after arriving. It seemed like forever, but she'd only been here a couple of days now. So many emotions had clouded her senses, she couldn't get past being targeted by these evil people. Could her sister's husband be that horrible?

"I hope the officers find something, anything, from my fingernails or my apron. And they did do whatever they do with a dust brush on the upstairs door."

"It takes time to get stuff like that back from the lab," Nathan said. "But meantime, we do what we have to do, ain't so?"

"*Ja*. And I'll be forever grateful for all you've done."

"That's what any friend would do."

Adina took in a deep breath and tried to calm her nerves, but she was just as nervous and aware of Nathan as she was of any criminals lurking about. "The air is different here."

Nathan glanced around, looking cute in a baseball cap instead of his straw work hat. "It's the ocean and the tropical breezes, fresh air. Not the same as Pennsylvania foothills and mountains, but *Gott*'s world still."

She lifted her hand. "And the palm trees, the flowers,

the banana trees. Bananas. I've never seen them hanging from the trees."

"I'll have to take you to Detwiler's Market," he said. "They have all kinds of fresh fruits and vegetables grown locally as well as anything else you'd need to make a meal." He grinned. "And the Sarasota Farmers Market is legendary around here. It's like a mud sale with an urban flare."

"What's an 'urban flare'?"

"City people who flock to booths full of fresh food—from bread to produce—and everything else you can think of—art, candles, clothing, home goods, treats, sweets and weird healthy stuff that pigs might not like."

She laughed at that. "That sounds *wunderbar gut.* I love to cook. Aenti didn't like me messing up her kitchen though."

"Your *aenti,* Rita, sounds like a difficult woman."

"That's an understatement."

The taxi pulled up and she noted the driver was a young *Englisch* man. He nodded and asked, "Where to?"

Nathan named the road. "It's east of here," he told the driver after they'd gotten in the back seat. "A few miles."

The driver gave him a frown. "I don't go over that way much. We call it the Meissner's Mirage. Swampy and off-limits to most."

"I'll pay extra," Nathan said. "We're doing a welfare check on a friend."

"Whatever, man." The driver took off. "But I'm not sticking around to find out what happens."

"Fine. I'll call you when we're done if you're willing to come back for us."

The driver grunted. "I don't want to leave anyone stranded. The best I can do is park at the main highway. You can walk the half mile through that swamp. My car might get stuck on that old rutty road. But I'll try to come back for you."

Nathan nodded. "*De*— Thank you." He'd almost slipped there.

Adina gave him a questioning glance.

"The house is in a secluded area," he told her on a low whisper. "I checked the map and talked to a few people. If there is anyone there, we won't be welcome."

"Maybe this is a fool's errand," she said. "I mean, we're not being very smart about it but I have to know, Nathan. I have to try."

Nathan studied the streets as the car buzzed through traffic. "You're right. Doing this goes against my better nature, and my friends at the police department will be displeased with us for risking this. But I understand the need to see what you can find here and hopefully get a clue as to where Blythe might be.

"We'll be careful," he said. "I'd hoped to drive by first, but that doesn't sound possible. If we don't like what we find, we'll leave."

She nodded, only because she didn't want him to get hurt.

Nathan pulled her close. "According to what we heard from the police, Meissner shouldn't be here. And I doubt he's got guards at his home all the time. The police told me the place is vacant right now, so at best we can look around the outside and who knows, maybe Blythe is hiding and will show herself."

Adina saw the earnest hope in his eyes. He was trying so much to help her. Nathan owed her nothing, but he was the kind of man who'd stand up for what he believed to be right.

Nathan sent her a reassuring glance then he took her

hand in his. She glanced down at his fingers intertwined with hers.

"Friends," she whispered as she held his gaze.

"Friends," he replied. "No matter what else."

Forty-five minutes later, after traffic delays and the driver getting lost twice, they found Mirage Drive.

"A fitting name," the driver said. "It seems to disappear into the trees."

Nathan couldn't argue with that. The sign was well hidden and the road was nothing but a sandy path between wild palmetto palms and massive old magnolia and pine trees. The foliage was so dense in places, he only saw green twisted vines choking away at the scrub oaks and swaying pines.

The driver turned to them after Nathan gave him a hefty amount of bills. "I'll wait for fifteen minutes, but if anyone pulls up behind me, I'm out of here."

"Fair enough," Nathan replied. "Thanks."

The driver laughed. "Man, it's obvious by your accents you're both Amish, but I'm cool with that."

"Then, *denke*," Nathan said without explanation. If this young man could see through their disguises, anyone else might do the same.

"Let's get in there and get out if we don't find Blythe," he said as they started walking up a sandy, shell-covered lane. "This place is creepy."

"*Ja*," Adina said, a visible shiver shaking her body. "I can't understand why Blythe would go on and on about her home here."

She did a thorough search on the ground after the taxi zoomed away. She'd been told back in town to watch for all kinds of creatures because of the creek running nearby.

Made sense to do so here, too. She didn't want to have a run-in with an alligator or a snake.

Nathan held her hand and glanced both ways along the path. After they'd walked about a half mile through palm trees and bamboo that stretched up to the sky, the sounds of animals running away all around them, the path took a curve back toward the sea.

And there stood the stark white house, two levels with porches running around each floor, the ocean crashing behind it as if to take it under, the seagulls cawing as if calling for help, the house still and quiet and waiting.

Adina gasped and then turned to Nathan. "I've never seen anything so beautiful…and so sad at the same time."

Nathan held her arm, the wind moving over them with a soft moan, mist from the sea spraying lightly against their skin.

"Melancholy," Adina said. "It's a melancholy place and I don't want to linger here too long."

"I agree. Let's see what we can find and quickly. Then we'll get back home, one way or another."

They hurried through the wind and the sand. Nathan checked for vehicles inside the open concrete bottom floor that served as a garage surrounded by huge pilings. Then he checked for carts and buggies, off-road equipment and even bicycles. Nothing.

A few storage buildings lined up near the dense property back toward the road, but the house looked deserted.

"Let's check the other side before we try any doors."

Adina moved with him, watchful, her eyes bright with curiosity and fear. "I can't believe Blythe lives here with no friends or any other Amish families around."

"It's fancy," he said. "And isolated."

"No wonder she was so miserable. Cut off from the

world in a paradise that must have become a prison. My poor sister."

Nathan could feel the empathy in her words. A perfect beach house in front of them, but with an evil pall over it, even here in this little bit of beauty. He thought of Blythe. Had she been forced to come here only to be taken away and gone forever?

He prayed not. He prayed they'd find some sort of hint to her whereabouts. He only hoped they didn't find her body.

What they found didn't bode well for Blythe.

Adina stood staring at a place that had to have been a beautiful home at one time. After circling the upstairs porch, they'd found an open door in the corner facing the water, the sheer white curtains lifting out in the wind like a warning wave.

Nathan went in through the open French door first, but Adina hurried to follow him into a large bedroom.

She gasped. "What happened here?"

Nathan held her back, but not before she saw the broken lamp, the messy blue-and-yellow flowered bed coverings and one lonely purple flip-flop by the open door. Adina held a hand to her mouth as she moved through the destruction of this room, a hint of her sister's favorite jasmine lotion teasing at her nose.

"Blythe?" she whispered. "Blythe?" When her whispers went unanswered, she cried out in a scream. "Blythe, where are you?"

Then the floodgate burst and she dropped to the floor and picked up the worn flip-flop and held it in her hand. Nathan kneeled beside her and pulled her into his arms.

"I'm sorry," he said, holding her there.

Adina went to him, tears falling for her lost parents, her

missing sister and her broken heart. She cried out, wishing someone would hear her.

Nathan lifted her chin, his gaze full of understanding and pain. "I'm here," he said. "I'm here."

She laid her head against his shoulder again and cried until she was spent, there in the once lovely room, all sunshine and sheers in shades of stark white, deep turquoise and seagrass mint, a pall of evil lifting over the air and the sound of the ocean crashing and purging as if the Lord cried along with her.

Finally, she lifted her head and wiped her eyes, then gazed at Nathan. "You are a special man to get involved in this."

He leaned in, his gaze soft and sincere, kind. "I only get involved with special women."

Adina drew in a quick breath, thinking he was going to kiss her. But a noise outside caused them to part and hurry to stand up. Adina straightened her shirt and pushed at her hair. Then she wiped her eyes and spotted something on the chair in the corner. A starfish-embossed scarf. Grabbing it, she tucked it in the pocket of the loose jeans she was wearing. For sentimental reasons, and because it had Blythe's scent on it.

Nathan pulled her back onto the porch and urged her to go to the front so they could get away. But too late, they spotted an off-road vehicle heading toward the house.

He pointed to the open door and they went back inside and down the stairs to find another way out. When he found a door that led down to the open ground-level area, he hurried her down the stairs.

"Run toward the road," he told her, pushing her ahead of him.

Adina took off, Nathan on her heels, the sound of the four-wheeler's motor roaring like a big bear.

"Hurry," he said. "Before they make the curve."

Then he motioned toward a small outbuilding to their right. "There, Adina. We can hide in there."

He forced open the rickety doors and shoved her in, then closed the door behind them and found an old bench to shove toward it. Dust and decay assaulted her senses, and cobwebs drifted across the slits between the old, rotting boards. She shivered as something did a fast skittle along her neck.

Nathan held her, his chest a solid protection against her fears. They were so close she could feel the warmth of him like a shield around her, keeping her secure and safe. She wanted to be his shield against the world, too. But right now, she could barely breathe from fear and exhaustion—and being so close to him. She had to remind herself that they were mere yards away from someone who'd have no qualms about killing them.

Outside, the four-wheeler crashed by within feet of where they'd just been running. Nathan tugged her close as they squeezed against a wall.

And then the motor went dead and they heard footsteps stomping over the crushed shells and rocks.

Footsteps headed directly toward them.

Nathan held Adina close and put a finger to his lips.

Then he pushed her into a corner where some old boards stood slanted against the creaky wall. "Hide under here."

"Not without you."

"I can't fit back there. I have to find something to protect you."

She pointed to some of the smaller wooden boards. "We can use these, not only to hide, but as weapons."

Adina was a smart woman, and right now he needed

some space between them because she was also a pretty woman with a floral scent that drew him like nectar. He had to focus on protecting her rather than kissing her.

"*Gut* suggestion," he whispered as he found a sturdy two-by-four that could fell a man if used in the right way. "You stay behind the boards and I'll take care of the rest."

"*Neh.*" She picked a small splintery board of her own. "You get on one side of the door and I'll be on the other side. I can trip him and you can nab him."

Nab? Nathan decided she read too many crime books, but her idea did have merit.

With no time to waste, he did as she said while they waited for the door to open. Then he quickly grabbed another board to silently wedge against the door. That would give them some time.

The footsteps went around the building, each crackle of plants being crushed growing closer and closer. Nathan could hear the person breathing heavily with each step, could sense the smell of a sweaty person. Whoever was out there was now making a shadow directly in front of them. He hoped the person couldn't see between the slats of wood. Nathan could only spot boots and dark pants from where he hovered near a rotten piece of lumber.

The intruder jiggled the door and then pushed at it. Finding it hard to open with the big bench jammed against it, he grunted and slammed his full body onto the door.

It seemed to give but it didn't open.

Nathan held tight to his board and checked Adina. She looked like some sort of avenging princess standing there with her board held low so she could trip up the intruder.

Then a phone rang, jarring them both. The person stepped away, his voice carrying over the air.

"Hello," the man said. Then, "I think someone—" He

must have been interrupted. He let out a grunt. "I'll be right there, sir."

They heard a swish of clothing and feet stomping away. The engine came to life again and Nathan let out a long breath.

"Is he gone?" Adina asked in a low whisper.

Nathan listened as the roar grew farther away. "I think so. Let's give it a couple of minutes and then we'll hurry to the road."

They waited there, not daring to move and barely breathing. He glanced at Adina off and on, giving her reassuring tight smiles. The woods and road settled down and he could almost feel the swamp taking over again, claiming nature again.

Within minutes they opened the door and he peeked out.

"Clear," he said, grabbing Adina's hand.

They took off running along the main road, staying as close to the dense weeds and bushes as possible. But when he stopped to call for the cab, they heard another roaring motor somewhere off in the distance.

"We might have to walk back toward town," he told Adina as they took off running to the highway. "We can't call our taxi back now."

"Whatever it takes to get away from here," she said on a breathless run. She held his hand and kept up with him until they were safely away from Meissner's Mirage.

Then she whispered, "Nathan, he had the same tattoo as the man who tried to take me."

SEVEN

They had to walk almost a mile before they found civilization again. Seeing people walking, biking and driving carts around here was normal, Nathan told Adina. They were dirty and tired and hot, but they looked like two lost tourists. Adina hoped that would bode well for them if anyone came snooping.

Nathan kept a watch on the road and the dense woods with beach homes and dunes scattered around them. Adina learned about seagrass and shrub thickets. She admired the beach morning glories and sunflowers, and the wild palmetto palms. They listened for humans and then he told her about pythons and alligators, and several different kinds of lizards.

"I might not ever want to take a walk again," Adina said, amazed at the beauty and the danger of this land. Her nerves tensed at the slightest movement, however.

Nathan told her, "Just be mindful. We had snakes back in Campton Creek, not to mention all kinds of other varmints."

"You're right. It's the human predators we have to worry about now."

She couldn't let her mind go past seeing that lone flip-flop there by the door of that ransacked bedroom. She didn't want to think of how terrified her sister must have been, or the reason a husband would do that to his own wife.

Nathan glanced over at her. "Hang on, Adina. Look, a place up ahead. I'll find us some water and try the taxi service again," he told her as they reached a convenience store not far from Sarasota proper and Pinecraft. "I shouldn't have brought you out here."

"I asked you to," she reminded him. "Now I know for sure something bad happened." She stopped, afraid she'd have another meltdown. "I have to keep trying. I'm hoping I can meet her friend, Clara, soon. Blythe needs me."

After Nathan got a taxi, they went inside the crowded store to buy two bottled waters. Then they waited outside, the noonday sun hot on their backs as they stood under two towering oaks.

"It did look as if she'd either ran out that door, or was forced out," he said, sympathy in his gaze. "I can't deny it, Adina. I'm worried."

"I know," she said. "I won't believe the worst until… until we have proof."

"So if Meissner is pretending to be searching for her, that could mean many things." Nathan took a swig of water and continued. "He either has her somewhere else or…she's been taken and he's trying to find her. Or course, he could have hidden her in plain sight."

"What do you mean? We checked the whole house."

"But we were only inside the bedroom where an obvious struggle took place."

"Which proves something is wrong."

"But why haven't the officials mentioned the struggle or secured that room with police tape?"

Adina thought about that for a moment, then let out a breath. "Because she was moved *after* they searched the house. The struggle could have happened after the police had left. He has her and he's hiding out with her. Or he could be running scared over something."

"That's what I'm thinking. He must have hidden her somewhere on the property and after the locals left, he brought her back to the house. The closets and cabinets in that room had been searched. Why would a man search his own home?"

"He's looking for something he needs?"

"*Ja*, and that could mean his men think you have something of Blythe's." Nathan glanced around again. "What would be so bad that he'd do this to his wife and you, her sister? What could Blythe have stumbled on?"

"I don't know," she said. "Why would I? I haven't seen her in months and when we did talk on the phone, she implied she was happy. When she suddenly stopped calling, I became concerned."

"They could think she told you some sort of secret."

"Again, she didn't. But she did seem to want me here."

They stood silent for a moment until Nathan spotted a slow-moving black economy car pulling into the busy, large parking lot.

"Adina, turn toward me."

"Why?"

He lifted his chin toward the car circling the store. "I think we have company and it's not our driver."

The car slowed as it passed close to them, the man had his window down. He studied the lot and all the people in it.

"The sea creature tattoo," Adina whispered, a hand to her face. "It's on his arm."

Nathan grabbed Adina and turned her around. "I'm going to kiss you," he said.

Before she could complain, he pulled her close then lifted her chin and kissed her, his lips gently grazing hers.

"We're pretending to be *Englisch*," he whispered. "So this has to look real." Then he kissed her again.

Adina knew the moment when the pretending ended and a real kiss began. Her heart pumped, her head became light, her feet seemed to want to leave the ground. Nathan's touch on her lips was sweet and enticing all at the same time. His kiss deepened each time their lips met.

When they heard the roar of a motor zooming on past, Nathan pulled back and looked down at her, a shocked expression on his face, along with a deep blush. Then he glanced toward the parking lot. "The car's gone and our ride is here."

Had she heard relief in that notification? Maybe he'd been pretending, but the way he'd held her and kissed her made Adina think differently. Would she ever understand this man?

"Nathan?"

Adina could feel the tension rising as he silently ushered her toward the taxi. He checked the driver, then helped her inside and told the driver to take them to Phillippi Creek.

Adina stayed quiet, her hand wanting to touch her lips. She gripped her fingers together to keep from doing that while she got her trembling emotions back to a calm level.

She ventured a glance over at Nathan. He stared straight ahead. He regretted kissing her. She could see it in the way he sat far across the seat from her, in the way he had one hand on the door and one on the seat between them.

She pulled away, too. Because she did not regret that kiss, not for one minute. They would have to be careful from now on. She didn't want to give him the wrong impression, because they'd only been pretending to protect themselves.

But the impression he'd left on her lips had been anything but pretending. She knew it, and so did he.

* * *

They returned home in silence, but the chemistry between them had changed and charged up to a high intensity.

Adina could tell his *mamm* had picked up on the tension. Ruth quietly fed them sandwiches and potato chips with tea cakes. Nathan had eaten like a starving man while Adina had nibbled her food like a frightened pony, her appetite gone.

"So it was that bad?" Ruth asked after she'd let them eat, her gaze encompassing both of them. "You both look tuckered out."

Adina nodded then told her what they'd found. "That room was like a crime scene, and I fear my sister is hurt... or worse."

Ruth put a hand to her throat. "So you found no one there?"

Nathan finally spoke. "Someone showed up, but we managed to leave before they spotted us," Nathan said. "We called a taxi after walking for a while. That's why we're so messy."

"Well, we have a washroom and, Adina, your clothes are all clean, even the ones Betty gave you."

"That's so thoughtful," Adina said, glancing over at Nathan. "I'll get cleaned up and work a half day at the shop. I'm not a very good employee to take time off on my second day of work."

His *mamm*'s frown held kindness. "Nonsense, you'll get washed up and you'll go upstairs and rest. You've been through so much since you arrived here. You need a few hours of quiet."

"I think you should rest," Nathan said. "It's been a long day."

"Work keeps me from thinking about this," Adina replied, her tone masking the hurt of his words. But he was right. She did need some time to think things through. Her sister was missing and could be dead, and she'd kissed Nathan like she'd never see him again. "But maybe a little nap would help with this headache. The heat got to me, I think."

"You do look pale," Ruth said, her gaze moving from Adina to Nathan. "And you both look tired. Why I let either of you go there is beyond me."

"She needed to know, Mamm," Nathan said, his eyes on Adina now, his expression softening with a resolve he must have been fighting. "I couldn't let her go alone."

The way he'd said that indicated he'd done his duty, and that was that.

Adina stood, her stool scraping across the floor. "I'm going to get cleaned up."

She rushed into the washroom and shut the door, then leaned against it, her fingers on her lips, her other hand on her heart. She'd been kissed for the first time in her life by a man who had been forced to protect her. Nathan didn't want to settle down and he sure didn't mean for that kiss to go so far.

But it had moved into her heart now, and she'd never let it go. She'd have to let him go, however.

And she wouldn't allow him to get hurt out of some sense of duty. She'd do what she'd come here to do.

Find her sister.

After Adina left the kitchen, Nathan was about to make a run for it and go to his office. In his mind, he kept slapping himself. What a *dummkopp* thing to do, kissing Adina. He'd only done it out of desperation to keep her safe. Or maybe not. Maybe he'd wanted to kiss her all along.

Because about halfway in, the kiss had changed and

grown from faking it, to a real deep and *wunderbar* kiss. It had been a while since he'd even wanted to kiss a woman. But wow, their kiss scorched a path throughout his system that left him weak as a kitten and more determined than a mule.

Now what was he to do about that?

He couldn't even look at the woman. If he did, she'd see his true feelings. The world would see him for what he truly was—a lonely man who pretended to be happy baching it. Well, he had been content living here single and free as a bachelor. While he'd visited with women friends and had meals with their families, nothing ever clicked. No one ever fit his idea of the person he wanted to spend his life with.

Until today.

Until that kiss.

They'd been forced together and they'd had to hide in that postage stamp of an old shed, and he could still smell her fresh summery scent. It surrounded him like a lit candle, clearing his mind of preconceived notions and sanctimonious ideas.

He had his hand on the office door, ready to sort through the thousand thoughts filling his head.

"Hold it right there," Mamm said, her hand firm on his arm.

"What are you not telling me, Nathan? What really happened while you two were at that house?"

Nathan could never hide anything from Mamm. "A man on an off-road vehicle almost saw us, but we hid in a shed and then we had to walk awhile to find water and a taxi."

"Okay, that's concerning."

"It was." He could be truthful about some things, so he described what they'd seen in the bedroom. "I fear the worst and deep down inside, Adina does, too. So I'm not sure how we handle this from here on out."

"You should report what you found. They'll fuss that you went on your own, but if the authorities have not seen what you found there, they need to know. Adina came here with a need to help her sister, and now we're involved. We can't stop this situation. I don't want harm to come to any of us, but *ja*, we have to find an end to this. If word gets out, I'll lose business and we can't afford that."

"I'm going to do my best to get to the truth," he said. "There's just so much more going on."

"Oh, you mean between you and Adina?"

A heated blush moved over his face. "I'm not sure I understand."

"An understatement at that."

"Mamm, what are you saying?"

"I can see, *sohn*. I probably can see what you don't."

"Then tell me."

"You and Adina are growing close, ain't so?"

Nathan couldn't deny that. "*Ja*, but that's to be expected. We knew each other and now she's here and I like her. I'm also determined to help her. What else can I do?"

Ruth let out a chuckle. "Keep us all alive, I reckon."

"I will do that."

"And be kind to her, Nathan. She's innocent."

"I'd never hurt Adina, Mamm."

"I know. But her heart is innocent. If you have feelings for her, that's fine by me. If you aren't sure, don't push things."

"I'm trying to avoid things," he said in gruff voice. "I can't be falling for her. We only need to find out what happened to Blythe and, good or bad, Adina will leave. Then we can get back to normal around here."

Then they heard the washroom door swinging again.

And Adina stood there with a towel in her hand, her gaze on him. Nathan could tell from her hurt expression, she'd probably heard most of this conversation.

EIGHT

"Adina?"

She turned and ran up the stairs, her footsteps pounding like rocks against his heart. Why had he said all those things, knowing she was in the next room?

"I think we had this talk a little too late," Ruth said, her expression full of both awe and concern. "You two seem about ready to either butt heads or grab each other and hold tight."

"It's not like that," Nathan said, even though it was exactly like that. Maybe the danger all around them had heightened their awareness of each other. He should apologize.

When he moved to go after her, Ruth held him back. "Let the girl be. She's had a lot happening in a short time. She was brave to come and search for her sister, but she is terrified, Nathan. And not just of what might be the outcome on her sister's disappearance. She's terrified of being alone, and if she loses Blythe, she will be that. I can't see her returning to live with Rita now that she's run from the man her *aenti* expected her to marry. She could be shunned and ridiculed. Which means she'll either stay here or have to start over again somewhere else. Still alone."

Nathan stood silent, remembering how he'd come to

her defense and said he'd marry her. "She won't be alone. I can't let that happen."

Ruth's knowing expression changed as a light colored her bright eyes. "That's what I thought."

Confused, Nathan shook his head. "I have to get cleaned up and I have some work to do. I wish you wouldn't talk in riddles, Mamm."

"No riddles here, Nathan. I can see it all very clearly. And soon, I pray you will, too."

He hurried to the washroom and ran cold water over his face, then scrubbed his skin with a clean rag. He couldn't tell his *mamm*, but he'd had a strong reaction to Adina from the first time he'd saved her from those men. And even though she'd only been here a few days, that reaction had turned into a true attraction. The kiss they'd shared had sealed that deal.

But you need to clear up this mess with Blythe, first, he told himself. Adina wouldn't be in a marrying mood if she couldn't find out what happened to Blythe. And if that was the worst, how would she feel about anything then?

He wouldn't let her be alone. Whether their feelings developed into the real thing, or even if she was devastated and pushed him away, Adina would be a great match for any man and he was the man standing here now. He was also the man who needed to marry.

His *mamm* already knew all of this, of course.

Now to get through these threats, find the truth about Blythe and get on with marrying a *gut* woman. A woman he'd known but for the most part, had ignored. Other than brief conversations or small talk back when they were young, he'd never moved any further with Adina.

Ach, vell. He'd made up for that with a kiss that had jarred him into reality.

Having decided how the rest of his life would go, he went on with work around the shop. His *mamm* had given Betty and her husband a huge freshly baked apple pie for staying with her earlier. And she'd made an extra one for supper while Betty and Paul watched the shop. Not a busy day and no strangers walking about. He checked the new safety equipment he'd worked on and hoped no one would try again to harm them.

He'd need a slice of pie before this day was over.

After waiting for a while, he went up to the top porch to check the doors of Adina's room. They still needed some finishing touches. But first, he wanted to see if she was in her room or resting in Mamm's room. He wouldn't disturb her.

He found her sitting in a rocking chair pulled close to the wall, staring out toward the distant sea.

"Adina?"

She glanced at him and then back to the water. "It's so far away. Now that I've seen the ocean up close, I'd like to go there again when things are better."

"I know. But we're near it and I hope that helps. The ocean is soothing." He sat down on the chair beside her. "I'm sorry about earlier."

Her gaze zoomed in on him, her azure eyes reminding him of sea glass sparkling in the sunshine. "You don't need to be sorry, Nathan. You want me gone. I can see that, and I don't blame you. Blythe troubled you when we were youths and now here I am, interrupting your routine, messing up your simple, quiet life. I'm worse than my sister, I think."

"*Absatz,*" he said, holding up his hand for her to stop. "You are you, Adina. A good person who has been caught in a bad situation. But I don't want you to think I'm ready to get you out of here."

"It sounded so," she replied, rocking away now. "If you think for one minute that kiss made me want to pine away for you, then you are wrong. You owe me no obligations."

Nathan wanted to say he did owe her since he'd offered to marry her and then he'd kissed her, and now he did want her to pine for him because he was for certain sure pining for her. What came next? Him acting like a lovesick sap? He might be willing to do that even.

But not until she was out of danger.

"I don't feel obligated. I feel—" He stopped talking and took a deep breath. "I want to keep you safe, Adina. After that and beyond whatever we find, I want you to know you will not be alone."

"I'm used to being alone." She stared out at the water again. "I miss Blythe and my parents. I wish my *aenti* truly loved me and had my best interest at heart, but I can almost understand her need to find husbands for us who can also take care of her. I don't want to wind up bitter and old and sad, Nathan. That's what alone would be like."

Then she stood and went to the porch railing. "But I don't expect you to make me happy. I gave up on that kind of contentment a long time ago. I know you pity me and I'm thankful that you've stepped up. But you don't have to worry about me. Once this is over, I'll figure out what's next."

Nathan moved to stand next to her. "I'd like to help you with that, too. The figuring things out part."

Her gaze widened in surprise, but with a definite skeptical glare. "Don't make promises you can't keep and don't make assumptions about me."

Adina whirled so fast, she bumped right into his arms. They stood there, eyeing each other for a moment or two. He wanted to kiss her again, and badly. But she'd bolt like a newborn lamb. So he just held her gently. "I'm not making any promises. And no assumptions. We're friends. Friends help each other."

"Well, from your attitude after we kissed, we need to stay friends. And that's all."

She was about to turn and go back inside when a shot rang out and a bullet hit the thick porch post next to her head.

Nathan let out a growl and then shoved her inside, slammed the near-finished doors shut, then slid down the wall, shielding Adina the best he could. "Are you okay?" he asked, winded and shaking with anger.

She pressed her head against his shoulder and bobbed her chin. "I'm fine. Just frightened."

Then she saw his arm and let out a yelp. "Nathan, you're bleeding."

He glanced at his clean shirt, now with a slit mark, a dark spot seeping through it. "I felt a sting. They tried to shoot you."

"*Neh*, not me," she said, her gaze on his wound. "I think they were trying to hurt you so they could take me."

Nathan lifted her away and then turned on his knees to check the area. "Well, now my next plan will go into effect."

"And what is your next plan?"

"We're going back to the police." Then he turned and sank down beside her. "And I'm going to warn everyone in the neighborhood that we've had intruders, and now shooters. If this keeps up, Mamm will have to shutter her shop for a while."

"*Neh*, I'll leave before I let that happen."

"You can't do that," he said too strongly. When she glared at him, he added, "It's too dangerous. Someone just shot at us. That's amping things up way too high."

"Well, they missed this time, thankfully." She stood and brushed off her hands. "Let's go right now. We need someone who can really help us or we'll be at this forever. And Blythe's life depends on us getting to the truth."

"So does yours," he reminded her. "This quest is becoming more than we can handle."

Adina saw the fear in his eyes. But she also saw something else. A deep abiding brightness that made her feel warm and safe, despite the danger all around them. She wouldn't let these evil criminals harm Nathan or Ruth. Right now, they were the only two people she could trust and she'd never forgive herself if someone hurt either of them.

They called another cab to take them to the station in downtown Sarasota. Nathan explained he'd done some work for an officer there named Jack Butler. Now he knew most of the people who worked the streets in Pinecraft.

"He'll be able to tell us what we should do next and hopefully, he can put a watch on our place."

He'd said *our place*, and in her heart, Adina knew that he was referring to Ruth's place. Not *their* place, as in him and Adina. There could be no them.

"I hope Ruth will be all right," she said, to stop the flutter in her stomach. Nathan had called a neighbor to come and sit with Ruth. And he'd left the baseball bat nearby.

"My *mamm* is a strong woman, and she's greatly vexed. A criminal would be sorely sorry if he messes with her right now. Besides, I set the shop alarm, which we rarely do. But these days, it's necessary and it's been thoroughly updated."

She wanted to apologize again, but that wouldn't change all the things that had happened to them. His arm was bandaged now—just a flesh wound. She tried not to think about how that bullet could have injured him or worse, killed him.

She had to find a way to the truth and that might mean doing some things on her own. One way or another and whether he liked it or not. She couldn't go on like this and neither could he.

Once they were in the station, they settled into a cubical and waited. The place bustled with activity. Phones rang, people called out orders, or asked questions as they walked from one office to another. Some dragged handcuffed, scruffy-looking people along with them. Crime kept people busy, she supposed.

Lieutenant Jack Butler was a tall, nice-looking man with dark brown eyes and hair the same color. He smiled at Nathan, then nodded to Adina after Nathan introduced her.

"I've been read in on this, Nathan," he said. "Missing person. Your sister, Blythe Meissner?" he asked Adina.

She nodded. "I came here to look for her and the officers who came to the house after I was attacked told us she'd gone missing. I fear the worst."

After Nathan gave the officer the full report, he added, "These people are targeting Adina. They have to think she knows something, or they don't want her to find her sister. The house was fine, except for the bedroom where an obvious struggle took place. And now this. He pointed to his arm."

Adina handed him the paper bag she'd brought. "I took a scarf from a chair in the room. My sister's scarf. I know you have dogs that can trace scents."

The lieutenant gave Nathan a glance and then showed admiration as he nodded at her. "We do. Smart thinking. Just like saving your apron and letting us scrape your fingernails."

"I read a lot of romantic suspense books."

"I see." Then he said, "You can help us more if you want."

"Gladly," Adina replied without hesitation.

"We'll have you look through a book of mug shots—photos. We need to prove the man we're holding is one of the two who tried to take you."

"I can do that," she said with a slight nod.

"And it might come down to you also identifying him in a lineup."

"You mean I'd be behind a two-way mirror and I see several different men who could be criminals?"

Jack chuckled. "You do know a bit about policing, but, Adina, don't believe everything you've read in books. In real life, things can get pretty nasty very quickly, and it takes more than a few days to crack a case."

"I understand," she retorted, "since I've been living this now rather than reading about such things."

"Fair enough," the officer said. "I'll let you look through the mug shots before you leave, and we'll see if he cracks before we bring you in for a lineup."

"What do you have so far?" Nathan asked his friend.

"We have the one man in custody and we're holding him on some outstanding warrants, but he's not talking," Butler said. "His fancy lawyer is working on getting him out on bail for a felony charge, but he'll have to go before a judge to make that happen, and that takes time. If he gets out and tries to skip, he'll be a wanted man all over this country."

"Do you think he can make bail?" Nathan asked.

"We're trying our best to avoid that, but you know how things work. We don't always get our way but if we have solid evidence that places him at your kidnapping scene or links him to someone we can pin down, we'll put him in a lineup and have you identify him. Until then, we follow the law and a judge's orders."

Jack glanced at the files again. "The man we're holding has a black octopus tattoo on his right arm."

"Near his wrist?" Adina asked. "I saw a tattoo on one of the men who grabbed me, and on the man on the off-road vehicle. I'm wondering if they all have one."

Jack's eyes went dark, his expression changed and the furrow on his forehead deepened. "Now we're getting somewhere."

Nathan leaned forward in his chair. "What does that mean?"

Jack shot him a quick glance. "We know this group well around here, too. Did you tell that in the original report, Adina?"

"Yes," she said, bobbing her head.

"Okay, that tidbit seems to have slipped through the mountain of paperwork we have around here. But…Meissner could have someone working inside to hide paperwork. I hope not, but that's always possible."

Adina lowered her head. "We could always be two steps behind them."

"I hope we get the DNA results soon," Nathan said, his words etched with frustration.

"That can take a while, but we might get a hit," the officer said. "Meantime, one, don't go back to that beach house. We'll send someone to check it over, because we now have probable cause to enter without a warrant. Two, stay together and watch your backs. I know you're already doing that, but you're both a target now. I'll put a patrol on the shop and your home. And three, you both seem to know a little bit about Hayden Meissner. So you can understand this is the real deal. We've had more complaints on that man, but we've never been able to nail him. If he's harmed his own wife, well, that's another thing."

Then he leaned close. "He seems to know things before anyone else hears them. The Black Octopus Company is known for being hired out to harass and intimidate people. And from what we've learned, Meissner is one of their best-paying clients."

Adina glanced around, wondering if someone here had tried to shoot Nathan an hour ago. "I don't think anyone saw us at the beach house, but that one man did come close to finding us."

"And the partner of the man in custody is still out there somewhere," Nathan said.

"We've got people watching for him, trust me," the officer said. "I'll send someone to check for bullet casings at your house, Nathan. And we'll definitely check the area around the Meissner place. He owns a lot of property around here. He could be hiding his wife on one of those properties."

They'd given his friend all the information they had. Adina found the man's photo in the mug shots almost immediately. Jack met with the other officers on the case and compared notes. "We have him on the scene and we have the tattoo to connect him to the others. I'll keep you both updated. Just be careful."

He offered them a patrol ride home and they took it. Word was out about the happenings, so Nathan told Adina he would alert the whole neighborhood. No one else needed to get hurt in all of this.

"I agree," she said, wishing she could make it all go away. She could only pray her way through this. "If I hadn't *kumm* to find Blythe, no one would know she's lost and needs to be found."

Nathan thanked the patrolman and hurried her into the shop. Ruth and her friend sat safe and sound, stitching away on some embroidery.

"We are fine," Ruth said before they could ask. "We've been watchful and I kept the alarms going. We didn't get many visitors and I locked the door each time anyone came in or left."

Relief filled Adina's soul. But she knew this was only the beginning. She'd somehow stumbled into something very dangerous. There would be more attacks. She could feel it in the air.

NINE

The next morning, Adina and Ruth were busy in the shop when an officer entered. Adina's heart plummeted to her feet. "Have you found my sister?" she asked as she rushed toward him.

Ruth finished up with her customer and once the shop was clear she joined Adina. "What's wrong, sir?"

The officer didn't offer his name and Adina didn't know his rank. He gave her a harsh glare. "We're still looking for Blythe Meissner. But in the meantime, we've had reports that you've been making some harsh comments about a prominent member of the Amish community. We take that very seriously down here, since we have so many Amish coming and going."

Ruth stared the man down. "I don't think it's against the law to file a complaint. You are aware that this young woman was almost kidnapped the night she arrived here, and my home and place of work have both had issues with people breaking in. My son has a wound on his arm from being shot at last night."

"I'm aware," the man said, moving farther in the room, his gaze dancing around. "That doesn't give you any proof to slander a fine man."

"And what fine man are you referring to?" Adina asked, her heart thumping while she boiled with anger.

"I think you know who we're all talking about," he replied. "Your slander needs to stop."

"What's your name?" Ruth asked, anger pinging through her question.

The officer's calm expression turned dark. "I don't need to give you a name. Just this warning. Stop with the assumptions."

"That will be enough."

They all turned to find Nathan standing in the door from the storeroom.

"I'm glad you showed up," the officer said. "You need to hear this. Let the police do the detective work. No more reports or suggestions about Hayden Meissner. Innocent until proven guilty, or don't you all know how that works?"

Nathan stepped forward and got between the man and his *mamm* and Adina. "I know how the law works. I also know that if anyone threatens any of us again, that person will regret it."

"You don't condone violence, do you?" the officer said, his hand settling on his gun holster.

"*Neh*, we don't," Nathan replied. "But I also don't condone a young woman being attacked and almost kidnapped, or my home being broken into, or a missing friend who can't be found. And I sure don't condone being shot at, not at all. You are not with the police department because I know most of the officers there. So either leave now, while you can, or I will call the real officer who checks on us every fifteen minutes and have you taken away—for threatening us."

The man only smiled and smirked. "You've been warned. You folks have a good day now."

Then he turned and walked out.

Nathan locked the door then whirled around. "Did he harm either of you?"

Adina shook her head. "*Neh.* We had him figured out. No real policeman would say those things to us."

Ruth nodded, taking Adina's hand. "She's correct. He's a fake. And you need to call the real authorities and report yet another threat."

"I will," Nathan said. "And I'll find out why the patrol watching us didn't alert us."

"It could have been an honest mistake," Ruth said. "He did have on an official-looking uniform."

Nathan watched the streets. "So he could still work there and he decided to take matters into his own hands, per the man who's really paying his salary."

"Hayden Meissner," Adina said, remembering what Lieutenant Butler had told them.

Nathan nodded. "I'm going to call and let them know and hope they can find their missing patrol. Or he could easily be in on this and gave this intruder the all clear."

"So many things to consider, so many people we can't trust," Ruth said. "Did you alert the neighbors?"

"That's where I've been for the last hour or so," Nathan replied. "We now have a high-alert neighborhood watch system in place. Several people I talked to complained about Hayden Meissner and his price-gouging ways. They're more than happy to help."

Adina and Ruth held onto each other. "Let's stay closed for now," Ruth said. "You and I will stay in and pray. That's what we need now more than anything—*Gott*'s intervention."

Adina agreed. The Lord had brought her here. He'd see her through. And she had Ruth and Nathan on her side.

She'd pray that they stayed safe, because right now they were the only people she had to help her—and she cared deeply about both of them.

The next day, Nathan told them the man who'd come to the shop was not known at the police department. "I described him and they showed me photos of all their current officers. He wasn't among them." He did a sweep of the streets, his gaze watchful. "He timed when the patrol would go around the block and come back, so he was able to get in and out before our guard even noticed. We'll have one out front, taking shifts, for twenty-four hours until further notice."

Ruth listened and stared at her son. "So this imposter is a dangerous man."

Nathan took off his hat and pushed at his hair. Adina had to swallow as she watched. He had nice brown hair with burnished threads shooting through it. While she focused on his hair, he let out a long huff of breath. "There's more. They showed me photos of former officers who'd left for various reasons."

"And?" Ruth asked, her gaze holding Nathan's.

"And I identified one of them as the man who came here yesterday."

Adina came to attention. "So he used to be a lawman?"

"*Ja*, but he got fired for breaking protocol and being too brutal during arrests. My friend Jack called him a hothead who wanted to do things his way."

"And now he works for Meissner," Adina finished. "That's sick."

"And he had the nerve to come here and threaten us," Ruth said, shaking her head. "But the right people are aware now, so that's that. We will open up and keep at our work.

I refuse to give in to fear. Nathan, I believe you have some outside work that you're behind on. We'll be fine here."

Adina glanced from Ruth to Nathan. "Just leave the baseball bat, okay?"

He smiled despite the concern in his eyes. "I do have a few things to finish up and I won't take on anything for the next few days. I've been assured you have a patrol guarding this property. And you have a phone, so keep it with you at all times."

"Did they find any bullet casings?" Adina asked, thinking this was not a typical conversation.

"They found the bullet," Nathan said. "Dug it out of the porch post. I think they can try to match it." He headed toward the back to his office. "Just be mindful. I'll work out back today. This place needs some trim work and stronger locks on the doors."

"I'm thankful we have wide chunky posts around this place," Ruth said to her after he'd closed the door. "Now, I need a cup of tea. The quilting club girls are coming early today. I don't want anyone here after dark."

Adina thought about that. "*Gut*. I wanted to ask them some questions about Blythe. I feel your friends know more than they are allowing."

Ruth pursed her lips. "You could be correct. We do tend to gossip a bit. And each time she came in, if they were here, they'd ask her about her life and living in a big home. She was always kind, but she seemed uncomfortable."

"And you've been kind by not talking about her," Adina said.

"I would offer you information, but I was usually busy helping other customers or doing things back in the kitchen. She rarely came in later in the day, but when she did and if they were here, they did talk to her. They weren't being nosy. I think they were more concerned."

"I appreciate that," Adina said. "So you won't mind if I ask them a few questions?"

"Not at all. I think anything can help at this point. I didn't want to bring it up with you because I didn't want hearsay to get in the way of the truth. Things are not always as they seem."

"I'm beginning to understand that," Adina replied. "Now, we have work to do. Staying busy keeps my mine off things."

"You are wise," Ruth replied, nodding her approval.

Adina spruced up the quilting table and made sure the needed supplies were close by. She admired the quilt the ladies had been working on. It was a starburst with the colors of the ocean—light sky blue to deep navy, turquoise and azure, as Ruth had called it. When finished, it would look like the heavens glistening over water. And in the very center—a stunning deep yellow that shined like the sun bursting to life.

She wanted to help create beautiful things such as this, but each time she got close to joy and hope, pain and guilt washed in afterward. What would she do if they never found Blythe? Would she ever know joy again?

Ruth walked up to her. "We have to hold out hope, Adina."

"Is it that obvious?" she asked, lowering her head.

"It's natural to worry and fret. You've had a tough time since your *mamm* passed, ain't so?"

Adina nodded. "I've never gotten over losing her and Daed."

"I know that feeling," Ruth admitted. "I worry for Nathan. I've prayed for him to find someone to love, someone to love him as a helpmate."

Adina couldn't look at Ruth. Nathan's *mamm* would see what was in her heart.

"You know, you'd make a perfect match for Nathan," Ruth said.

Shocked, Adina lifted her head to respond, but the bells on the door jingled and in came Betty, Diane and Ellen, all smiles and chatter. Adina gulped in a breath, thankful for the reprieve.

Ruth gave her a quick smile while she waved to her friends. "Think about that." Then she turned and greeted her friends while Adina did think about that.

These days, besides worrying for her sister, Nathan was all she thought about. Now Ruth was playing matchmaker?

Nathan had spouted a proposal that he didn't really mean. Plus, he'd regretted kissing her and had made it clear he wasn't ready to settle down. She had implied the same, but her heart pleaded for a different want.

Where in there could there be any kind of match?

Ruth went to the kitchen to work on refreshments, and probably to give Adina a chance to talk to her friends about her sister.

"Oh, Blythe is a dear girl," Ellen said as she stitched away, her needle dancing along, the thread shifting like an unbreakable spiderweb. "She was always smiling and laughing, and she wore the prettiest dresses, in all colors of the rainbow."

"She loves her flip-flops," Betty said. "She had those in all the colors, too. And sneakers. The girl had so many shoes."

"She loves shoes," Adina said, noticing they switched from past to present tense when they caught it. Did they think her sister was dead? She almost told them about the lone flip-flop she'd found at the house, but no one knew she'd been there and it needed to stay that way.

Diane had been quiet. "Clara was supposed to *kumm* by and visit with you, but she's been busy with work. She wants to help in any way she can."

"I'd appreciate that," Adina replied. "I haven't had a moment to talk with Clara. But the more I know, the more I can put together a timeline and figure out where my sister might be. No one has heard from her or her husband for days now."

Helen leaned close. "I can tell you Blythe's pretty high-minded. She had a maid *kumm* twice a week to that house. And she had plenty of spending money. She'd buy whatever she wanted, but these last few weeks, your sister looked ill, and she didn't talk as much."

Adina stopped her stitching. "If she's ill, she could be somewhere in a hospital. I never thought of that. I can ask around."

Diane glanced at the clock and then the street, as if searching. "Clara did tell me that Hayden is beside himself, and he refuses to come home. He'd been out there searching, so if she was found in a hospital he'd know it by now. Even sent someone up north to see if she went back there."

Adina knew then she'd be hearing from Aenti Rita soon. If she'd found out Blythe truly was in trouble, she'd figure Adina was here. Aenti might show up, demanding Adina come home.

But Adina wasn't going back to Campton Creek. Ever. She'd just now decided that, but it was a relief to admit it to herself.

She'd stay here, hoping to see her sister again. Then they could have a life of their own. But a horrible thought hit her in her stomach, making her cringe with fear.

Hayden Meissner would never let Blythe go. Amish stayed married whether they stayed together or not.

The only way Blythe would be completely free was if she became a widow. But the man she'd married would never let that happen either. So if she'd been in a local hospital, Hayden would have found her by now. And he might have her hidden away and he could keep her hidden for as long as he wanted.

Diane looked as if she had more to say. "Adina, I don't want to get your hopes up, but Clara thought she saw someone who looked like Blythe in a local park only a few days ago."

Adina took in a breath. "Really?"

"I can't be sure," Diane said. "And Clara can be dramatic sometimes. But maybe someone could check there?"

"I'll definitely let the police know that. Would Clara be willing to talk to them about what she knows?"

"I'll ask when I get home," Diane replied. "We hope you hear something soon. The whole community is concerned about these people roaming about and threatening Nathan and Ruth."

"Because of me," Adina replied, wishing that wasn't true.

"*Neh*," Betty interjected. "Because of these bad people. You came with good intentions. And frankly, if you hadn't, everyone would go on with their lives. Some would be worried like we are, but the people who can help with this might not make much of it. You brought this situation to everyone's attention. Now we're all aware and watching for Blythe, and Clara's possible spotting of her is a good example of how we can help. Hayden Meissner is a powerful man, but we have the power of community and prayer on our side."

"*Denke*," Adina said. "You are all very kind."

"You are one of us," Betty replied. "I'm glad you're here. Ruth can use some help and you seem capable."

They took turns checking on the guard who walked back and forth outside. But other than that, today seemed like a normal day.

Adina knew that wouldn't last. She could feel it in her bones. Why would these people give up now? If Hayden needed to speak to her, he should come here himself.

Diane told her Blythe used to like to walk the shoreline of the park near Hayden's property. Adina would continue to try and question Clara and then she'd go to Blythe's favorite spot at the big park on the bay leading out to the Gulf. But she'd need someone to go with her.

Should she ask a patrolman or just go herself first? Would Nathan be willing to help her yet again? She'd ask. It was a long shot, but she only had a few opportunities to search on her own. She had to consider all the information she'd heard and go from there. Each day that went past meant another day of wondering.

TEN

The next day Nathan came into the kitchen and rubbed his sleepy eyes before he headed to the *kaffe* pot.

Adina sat drinking a strong cup of black tea laced with local honey and fresh lemon slices, but she glanced up when he entered. He always smelled so clean and fresh in the early morning.

"Hi," she said, forcing her gaze back on the devotional book Ruth had given her.

"Morning." He yawned and stretched, showing her muscles she'd not seen before.

"Did you keep watch again?"

"I tried. I know we have shifts coming in around the clock, but night worries me. Easy for someone to sneak in. Even with the alarm and the extra locks, I worry."

"I wish you didn't have to do these things."

"I know, but we're in it now. And things have been quiet for a couple of days at least."

She'd planned to ask him to go to the waterside park near the Meissner property with her, and she couldn't wait any longer. She'd gotten up early to check all the hospitals and walk-in clinics. After giving her sister's description, she couldn't find anyone who'd remembered Blythe, and they refused to give her any private patient information. The name didn't even bring about any recollections. Or people weren't telling her the truth. And she'd already attempted to meet Clara Kemp, who might know Blythe better than anyone. Diane had told her Clara had a day off on Friday. Adina didn't want to wait but she had no other choice right now.

"What are you thinking?"

She looked up from her toast to find Nathan standing there with a cup of *kaffe*, staring at her. "I need to go to a popular park where Blythe hung out and ask people there if they've seen her. Little Dove Park, I believe is the name. From what the quilting ladies told me, she went there a lot since it was close to their house and on the water. She liked to walk through the park and she often walked along the shores of the bay. One of your *mamm*'s friends has a daughter who might have seen her there. I'm going there if I have to hire a cab, but if you'd like to *kumm*—"

"What time do we leave?"

"You'll go, even with all the danger?"

"I'm as restless as you are, Adina. It will give us a break from hiding out here, and we'll get an officer to take us. He can walk a few feet behind us."

"*Gut* idea because they need to know that someone thought they'd spotted Blythe there, but I haven't been able to talk to the woman yet," she said, relaxing. "Clara Kemp. She knew Blythe. Do you know Clara?"

"I don't," he admitted. "She's Diane's only daughter still at home. She stayed after her father passed two years ago. That's all I really know about her, other than Diane's hints of finding Clara a husband. They have a large family and her two other married daughters tend to come and go. Most of them don't live here year-round."

"Diane said Clara has a job at a local bakery, but she takes a bus to get there. It's not within walking distance."

"We can find Clara later," he suggested. "This needs to be a quick trip to the park, and I'll make sure Mamm isn't alone when we go. Jack told me he'd have someone over here if anyone was left here alone. I'll call him after breakfast."

"*Denke*," Adina said. "You've been so kind to me, Nathan."

He stood there, his gaze holding her, his eyes full of so many emotions. "If we weren't under constant attack, I for certain sure would enjoy having you here. When this is over, I'll make amends and really show you around."

Adina couldn't look beyond searching. But she bobbed her head. "I'd like that."

"You two look mighty cozy," Ruth said as she rounded the stairs. "What are you plotting so early in the morning?"

"We're going to a park," Nathan explained. "One where Blythe often walked."

Ruth stopped, her tennis shoes squeaking. "Is that wise?"

"I'm going to get a patrol person to give us a ride," Nathan explained. "Jack told me he'd send someone to get us around town if needed, to keep us safe. And I'll make sure you have one here while we're gone."

"I see you've thought this through," Ruth replied, a trace of smugness mixed in with her worried expression. "It will do you good to get some fresh air, but *ja*, be careful. Just because things have been quiet doesn't mean this is over."

Nathan assured her they'd take care. He went into the office to call his friend.

"I just need to see the park," Adina said in her defense. "I can't stay hidden away forever. And if Hayden did go to Campton Creek to look for Blythe, he'll surely talk to

Aenti Rita. That means she'll either want me to come back home, or she'll show up here thinking to bring me home. I have to do something, anything."

"I understand," Ruth replied. "We must go on with our lives. We're not to live in a spirit of fear."

"And yet, I do," Adina admitted. "I don't like that."

"I agree," Ruth said. "While you're out, think on what I said yesterday."

"I've thought about that a lot," Adina replied. "Your son is a *wunderbar gut* man, Ruth. He deserves the best."

"And you don't believe you're the best? Do you think I try this with every woman he meets?"

"I hope not."

Ruth chuckled. "You're the first I ever even considered this much, but it's because of the way he glances at you and, well, because you just seem to belong here. I like your company, at that." Ruth's gaze held a melancholy hope. "Nan would be so happy for you and my Nathan to make a match."

Adina smiled a real smile for the first time in days. "I like it here and I love helping you in the shop. I know Mamm would approve of that. Aenti, not so much."

"Then I'll keep you around, whether my son agrees or not. He'll *kumm* to his senses in his own *gut* time, trust me."

"I do trust you—both of you," Adina said. "I only hope this can end soon. I need a true vacation."

"Don't we all."

Nathan returned and must have noticed the secretive vibes in the room. He studied their faces, his eyebrows lifting. "Jack is going to send an undercover officer as our escort. Not as blatant and hard to spot. I know the man and he's the best at his job. He'll be in the park watching us at all times."

"Maybe this can work to draw one of them out," Adina said. "I'm willing to take that risk."

"I don't like this, but I do understand you must do what needs to be done," Ruth replied. "Please be careful."

By the time Nathan had their trip arranged, Ruth and Adina were both walking around with a new hope hidden underneath the tension of still being targets. And poor Nathan had no idea what was stewing behind his back.

Or maybe, from the way he smiled at Adina, he did. But none of them could voice their hopes right now. Going to the park was just another means of seeking Blythe, and yet another dangerous risk that might backfire.

The undercover officer had dressed Amish. Adina learned his name was Simon Beiler but he told her everyone called him Simms.

Then he surprised her. "I used to be Amish," he said in a husky low voice. "But not anymore."

She didn't ask why. He must have his own reasons for jumping the fence. "*Denke*," she said instead. "For helping us."

"I don't like Hayden Meissner," he growled. "And I don't like men who hurt women."

Adina didn't argue with that reasoning and she wouldn't press him for his story. Even though he'd dressed Amish, she could see he'd become part of the *Englisch* world. His hair was shaggy but well cut and his dark blue eyes rivaled the night sky over the ocean. An interesting man and one she felt immediately safe being around.

She noticed the unmarked car that had a taxi sign slapped on its doors, and once she was nestled in the back seat with Nathan, a sense of security surrounded her.

"At least the weather is *gut*," Nathan said, his smile tentative. "Another adventure with Adina."

"Are you sure about this?" she asked, worry now clouding over her secure feelings. "I could have done it alone."

"*Neh*, and you know I wouldn't let you do that. I told you, you are not alone now."

"So we can walk around, seek out people who look like locals. I don't know, really."

Simms glanced back at them. "Nathan, you understand I know a lot of locals. I have certain people—confidential informants—who tell me things and some of them know this particular park. Some are homeless and practically live there. But I'll do the speaking to them today. You don't need to know who they are."

"Did you know Blythe?" Adina asked, hoping.

"I don't know her," Simms replied, emphasizing the word *don't*. "I do know a lot about her husband, however. He's no more Amish than I am even though he puts on the *pillar of the community* facade. I've wanted to catch him for a long time. When Lieutenant Butler told me what's been going on, I volunteered to help. Would have done so sooner, but I was working on a drug bust."

Adina figured he'd taken care of that situation. "I appreciate your help. It's not like Blythe to go silent on me."

"Ghosting you," Simms said as he maneuvered through traffic. "I find it odd that Meissner is hiding out, too. If he's so worried about her or even if someone else has her, why not show his face and ask for help?"

"I agree," Nathan said. "He's a private man and few people know where he is right now. I'd think he'd want to talk to Adina, rather than send people to harm her."

"He's sending people because he's hiding something," Simms replied. "Including his wife. I think she saw or heard something she wasn't supposed to know. So he's hiding her, or he's harmed her."

"I feel the same," Adina said. "That's why I'm here."

"And now, he wants to take care of you. He won't like you checking on her."

Simms didn't mince words.

"I think so. And he also wants Nathan out of the way so he can easily get to me."

"You've certainly figured all of this out," Simms said, giving her an admiring glance. "Don't get too bold, okay?"

"I won't," she said, thinking she'd do what needed to be done.

She glanced at Nathan. He gave her a grim stare, but he held her hand until they reached the big park.

Simms stopped the car in a packed sand parking lot near several other vehicles. "You two go on your walk. Act natural and enjoy the day. I'll be walking behind you, observing, protecting, and stopping here and there to ask people about Blythe. If I find someone who knows anything, I'll send Nathan a text."

They all got out of the vehicle and Adina took in the beautiful trees, manicured walking paths showcasing blooming flowers and the big bay gleaming in a sparkling pure blue. Birds of all sizes and shapes cawed and fluttered their wings, people laughed and walked by with their dogs or rode by on bikes. Children giggled on the playground.

But her mind was on her sister. Blythe had walked this path, had heard these same sounds and saw that same big beautiful body of water. Would she find some answers here today?

Nathan studied their surroundings. Palm trees and sand dunes, tall grasses and banana trees, oleander and hibiscus, azaleas and lilies, and beautiful magnolias. Several trails moved through the heavy overgrowth at the front of the property and a moist sandy walking path sliced along the shore. They'd taken off their shoes and held them, letting the warm water lap at their feet. This could be a nice walk if he didn't feel as if someone was after them.

He glanced back and saw Simms talking to a couple they'd seen earlier, lounging in two beach chairs. An older couple walked by with a little dog that barked at anything that moved.

Up ahead, a blue heron slowly made its way along the shore, searching for food. Seagulls lifted in the wind, flying out over the water.

"This is beautiful," Adina said. "I can see why Blythe would come here."

Nathan looked to the southeast. "Meissner's land is not far from here. I'm guessing it ends where the park proper begins. But it's a heavy jungle of pines and palmetto bushes, not to mention hundreds of other thickets. Hard to get through."

"Maybe she walked the shore from their place until she got here where she could breathe and feel free," Adina said, glancing into the thick twisted foliage on their left. "She might have run away, coming through here."

"That would make sense, if she knew the way to the park and could get here by foot."

"It never occurred to me that she might have left him, Nathan. If she feared for her life and escaped, maybe he *is* out there looking for her. But for all the wrong reasons."

"And she could be hiding in plain sight."

"Let's see how close we can get to his property," Adina suggested, her nerves on fire while a sheen of sweat broke out on her spine. "If she left a trail, we might find some clues."

"Anything she might have left if she did come here would be washed away by now," Nathan said. "The ocean takes back what the waves and tides bring in."

Adina kept walking, edging closer and closer to the dense interior of the wild forest. When they made it around a big curve, they both stopped.

"We need to go back," Nathan cautioned. "I don't see Simms and there's nothing here but snakes and probably some mean gators."

Adina went to turn when something caught her eye on the water's edge. "Nathan, look. Is that—"

Nathan grabbed her to keep her from running ahead. "We should go, Adina."

"*Neh.*" She pulled away. "I have to see. I have to know."

He hurried after her as she rushed to what looked like a body floating in the shallows by an outcropping of mangrove trees. If that was Blythe's body floating there, Nathan did not want Adina to see it. But too late. She didn't stop running until she was upon the body. And then she let out a scream.

ELEVEN

Adina gulped, sobs escaping with each breath. "It's not her. It's not Blythe."

Nathan held her back, trying to protect her from the grotesque body lifting with the tides. "It's a male."

Adina studied the corpse bobbing against the lapping waves. Then she blinked. "I think I've seen this man before. He was the first man—that night when they tried to take me. He…he has the tattoo, Nathan. The sea creature."

Nathan pulled her back while he stepped forward and saw the shape of a curling angry black octopus covering most of the man's lower arm. "You could be right. It's an unusual design. The Black Octopus Company."

"It's him," she said on a wobbly whisper. "Why is one of Meissner's men dead?"

"Because we *aren't* dead," Nathan replied. "He didn't do his job. I need to call Simms."

Adina nodded then moved away. She looked pale, apprehension shadowing her pretty face like a looming cloud. "I hope Blythe was able to get away. I pray that she's safe and away, and that she is getting help somehow."

Nathan touched a hand to her cheek. "I pray so, too."

He let Simms know where they were and what they'd found, then he took Adina a few yards back up the path to wait. Simms said he'd need their statement, but he'd have an officer take it so he didn't blow his cover. He'd meet up with them in a few.

Nathan held Adina there on the old driftwood log, his arm around her waist. She shivered and he pulled her closer still. "You're not alone in this. *Gott* brought you here for a reason, Adina. And I'm here for that same reason."

She turned to him as sirens screamed up in the park, startling both humans and the birds. "I know that now."

Then she laid her head against his shoulder and stared at the beautiful sea. "You're right about the ocean, Nathan. It takes back what the tide washes in, one way or another."

Nathan hated hearing the defeat in her words. "This man was a criminal, and while I wished him no harm, he chose this way of life. Meissner is an evil man who covers his crimes with a facade that has people believing him. Like a false prophet, he is not a man of *Gott*. Someone has to stop him."

"I think Blythe tried to do that and now—"

"We will find her. Simms is back in town and he's one of the best. I've done some work for him before, and he's not much on chitchat, but he has a kind streak in the way he watches over the Amish here. We Amish don't tend to get mixed up in these situations unless we're forced to do so. Finding justice is not a sin. It's necessary because this man is taking advantage of his own people, and the wife who promised to love him."

Adina burrowed closer. "I'm so cold."

"I'll get you home soon," he promised. Then he kissed the top of her head, his lips touching her crisp *kapp*. "Hang on, okay?"

She nodded then looked past him. "I see an officer hurrying this way."

They both stood as the uniformed patrol came toward them. Nathan explained and pointed to the man in the water. The officer went to check on the corpse. Then he called it in.

"I'll need to go over your statements," he told them. "Separately."

Nathan glanced at Adina. "I'll be right over here, okay?"

She nodded and held herself against the driftwood log they'd been seated on. Then she turned her gaze back to the water.

He hurried through his explanation. "We came to the park for a break and decided to walk the shore. We were about to turn back when we saw someone at the water's edge. That man."

"Do you know the man?"

More explanations. "My friend Adina came here to look for her sister." He gave the officer all of their names. "We'd heard she used to frequent this park because it's near her husband's land. We believe this man worked for the Meissners because we saw him a few days ago near their beach house." He explained about the tattoo. "She saw that same tattoo on the man who first tried to abduct her, so we believe this could be that man."

"And you conveniently found him floating in the water today?"

"Nothing convenient about finding someone dead, Officer. We came here looking for answers to where Blythe Meissner might be, and I think we found one answer. This man didn't do his job. He didn't bring Adina to Meissner."

"You have no proof of that, right?"

"*Neh*, we do not." He retold the whole story, wondering why some of the officers doubted them. "Simms is on the case now, as you well know. Talk to him about the how and why of this. I need to get Adina home."

The officer went over to her and asked her the same questions, leaving her even more shaken. Nathan listened from a few feet away, hoping this would get the locals even more involved.

The officer called for backup and an ambulance.

"You two go back to the park where Simms is waiting. If we have more questions, you can come to the station."

They did as he said, Nathan holding on to Adina's arm. She was drained and she'd seen a horrible thing—a body floating in the water, days old at that. Not a sight anyone wanted to remember. But especially upsetting, considering this same man had tried to harm her a few days ago.

Simms stalked toward them, his frown making him look formidable as he tilted his head toward Nathan. "You two lost me, man."

"We got carried away with getting to Meissner's property," Nathan said. "I checked back when you were talking to someone."

Simms let out a sigh. "Well, at least you did find something. I got nowhere with the few people hanging out today. I'm guessing Meissner offed one of his own for not following through."

"That's what we think, too," Nathan said. "If we hadn't found him, he might have gone back out to sea or someone else would have seen him and it would have taken more time to connect him to this case."

Simms did a little stroll, his hands on his hips. "You two are worrisome already. You don't need to go off like some kind of Amish mafia seeking justice."

Adina pulled away from Nathan and got right into Simms's face. Or more like his chest since she wasn't tall enough to meet him at eye level.

"Seeking justice is what needs to be done," she said, her

voice rising. "My sister has been missing for weeks now as far as I can tell and I came here to find her. I got attacked, almost kidnapped, shot at and Nathan's home was broken into because of me. He was shot at because of me. And no one has found her or even considered finding this Meissner person—her husband. So don't tell me to stop asking questions, or to stop looking for Blythe. If I hear that one more time, I'm going to scream. You're supposed to be *gut* at your job, *ja*? So do your job, please. Just do your job for us, for your friend, Nathan. For Blythe. We stumbled on a body and now we're getting a lecture. Really?"

Nathan pulled her back while Simms stood there silent and still, his midnight eyes full of awe. Then his friend nodded. "Yes, ma'am. Got it. I'll find Blythe. I promise."

Adina lowered her head and let out a breath. Then she turned to Nathan, her body shivering. "Take me home."

Nathan tugged her close. "Should I call a cab?" he asked Simms.

"Nope." Simms did a circle with his finger. "I brought you here so I'll deliver you home. And then I'll get right back to this new development. We've got one sitting this out in jail, and now one dead. And they are both with the Black Octopus Company. Meissner will get sloppy and mess up and I'll be there to haul him in."

Adina gave him a hard stare and then walked around him. But she pivoted, causing Nathan and Simms to stop. "*Denke*," she said in her sweet voice. "I will pray for you."

"I do believe that," Simms whispered to Nathan, rolling his eyes. "And…I do appreciate your prayers." Then he patted Nathan's shoulder. "I'll do the same for you, my friend. I think you will definitely need lots of prayers with that one."

Once they were back home the sun was dipping lower on the horizon. Adina collapsed on the small couch in the kitchen and put her hands to her eyes. "It was horrible, Ruth. So horrible."

Ruth sent Nathan a worried glance that Adina caught when she looked up. "And I was rude to Simms. I'm so ashamed."

"We'll bake Simms a pecan pie," Ruth said. "He's seen worse, for certain sure."

"But he was there, putting his life on the line for me," Adina said. "And what did I do? I had a tantrum and told him what for."

"He might have needed a *gut* talking-to," Ruth replied, as serene as ever. "Let's not dwell on Simms. He's a capable man. I'm more worried about you right now."

Adina lifted her spine and wiped her eyes. "I will personally bake that pie." Then she stood. "We found one of them there in the water—dead. The other is in jail and refusing to talk. But that third one, the one we saw on the off-road vehicle is still out there. We can't find Blythe until we find Meissner."

"What are you saying?" Nathan asked with caution. "We can't be anywhere near Meissner."

"I'm not going after Meissner," Adina replied, her heartbeat finally slowing. "But I hope Simms will search for him, and soon. If he's not too angry at me."

Nathan shook his head. "Simms is angry at the world. But he is a *gut* man and he's very thorough on finding criminals."

Adina studied Nathan for a moment. "How did you get so friendly with the authorities anyway?"

Ruth held up her hand. "I can answer that. You know when I asked you how you knew so much about protecting yourself and you said because you had to learn?"

Adina nodded.

"Well, after Nathan's *daed* passed, I was alone and afraid. Nathan went to the local station and asked them to watch out for me until he could get here permanently. He didn't trust anyone much. But he was concerned with me running a business on my own."

Ruth shrugged. "I had to learn, too. I had to learn to be alone, and if need be, to protect myself. That baseball bat was once mine. I kept it by my bed at night and now we keep it near the shop. A suggestion from Simms himself." She held her hand near her mouth and whispered loud, "He used to be Amish."

"He actually told me that." Adina looked over at Nathan. "I'd expect no less from you. Wanting to protect everyone seems to be your goal."

Nathan shrugged just as Ruth had. "What can I say? She's my *mamm*. And for the record, I met Simms first. He came into Dawson's a lot and Tanner Dawson told him I did handiwork. He hired me to help him build a dock and a deck. He has a small cottage on the bay. When he's home, that is."

Adina was learning more and more about this family. Tight-knit, loving, protective. She'd had none of those things after her parents died. She and Blythe had become a burden to her *aenti*. And they had no one else.

"I'm glad you found friends to help," she said. "I will always be grateful for what you've done for me."

"You are family now," Ruth said. She glanced toward her son.

"*Ja*, you are family now, Adina," he said. "Even after this is over, no matter the outcome. I told you, you'd never be alone again and I meant that."

Adina nodded. "I can never thank either of you enough. I'm going to freshen up and then I'll help with supper."

Ruth smiled and then said, "Oh, by the way, Clara came by while you were gone. She said she'd be back tomorrow. She is concerned, of course."

That caught Adina's attention. "Finally, someone who might shed some light on what's going on. I hope Clara can answer some of my questions. And maybe she will have news on where Hayden Meissner is, too." She stood there, her head down. "I fear he has taken Blythe and left this area, or worse, taken her so far away I'll never see her again. I can't think beyond that."

Then she turned and headed upstairs before she started crying again. When she got to her room, she saw the butterfly embossed backpack her sister had sent her just a few months ago. Grabbing it, she held it close and dreamed of happier days when Mamm and Daed were alive and well and laughing. They'd dance with their daughters and sing silly songs. They'd chase butterflies and pretend they could fly, too.

How she longed for silly songs and butterflies.

She could cry into her pillow but she had to stay strong for Nathan and Ruth. And for Blythe, too. She prayed they'd be together once again and they could sing all the songs they wanted. Adina went to the new doors and stared out at the palm fronds lifting in the wind. The streetlights made the whole street look ethereal.

Then she spotted a lone figure standing just down the way, staring toward the house.

TWELVE

Adina slipped back out of view, a gasp caught in her throat. These people might not try to break in again, but they were watching. Even with patrol people walking around and circling the block, Meissner kept sending his henchmen to do damage.

Her first inclination was to open the door, run down the stairs and confront the man, hoping the authorities would see.

But that would be *lecherich*. All of this was ridiculous in a cruel, sinister way. She prayed it could end soon.

Adina whirled and hurried downstairs to find that baseball bat. But instead, she found Nathan.

"I saw someone outside," he said, one foot on the bottom stair. "I'm guessing you did, too."

She nodded. "I was looking for your bat."

He shook his head. "*Neh,* you are not going to go out there."

"But—"

"But I've notified the patrol. I'm waiting to see what happens next."

Adina sagged in relief. "Do you ever rest?"

"Not much."

He went to the window and peeked through the blinds. "The man is gone. I hope he saw the patrol and took a hike."

"He can hike back," she pointed out, wondering if she'd be looking over her shoulder for the rest of her life.

"Do you know how to swim?" Nathan asked as he turned back to her.

The question was so serious, she had to answer. "I do. You remember back home Jeremiah Weaver teaches Amish how to swim?"

"*Ja.* I already know how, but he does it because his best friend died in the creek, right?"

"That and his stepdaughter almost drowned there before he was even married to Ava Jane. Now, why do you ask that question?"

Nathan shook his head. "I don't know. A feeling. With all the water around here."

Adina shivered again, the memory of that man floating so lifeless still fresh in her mind. "You're afraid Blythe might be in the ocean?"

"I didn't say that."

"But that's what happens to people here?"

"I didn't say that either. Just seeing what we found today made me fear something could happen to you. Something bad. If you were near water, you could try to swim away."

"I've had that fear since I arrived, Nathan. But water or not, I'll find a way to save myself."

He tugged her close. "I have that fear for you, but now it's worse. Now I don't want you to leave, but I also don't want you to get hurt by being here."

Adina looked into his eyes. She shouldn't feel this way because she might *have* to leave. Her *aenti* could come and try to force her home to marry Elman Barr. Or as they both feared, Adina could meet Blythe's fate and what if that led to Nathan and Ruth being hurt?

"I'll have to leave one day," she said, thinking he might

feel like her protector now but he could come to resent her if this didn't end soon. "You're only being kind."

He gave her an odd stare, as if he was surprised. "You think I'd just let you go back to Campton Creek, after all of this?"

She was about to answer him when they heard a scream coming from Ruth's room. Nathan ran past Adina and hurried up the stairs. Adina followed, rushing into Ruth's room to find his mother on the floor moaning, her forehead covered in blood.

Nathan sat in the emergency room waiting to hear about his mother's injury. Adina paced beside him, walking a path over the fake wood floors, her sneakers squeaking each time she pivoted and started again.

His *mamm* had been hit over the head with what she believed to be a heavy piece of wood. Stray wood, she called it, telling Nathan someone must have pulled it out of a trash pile.

He finally stood and stopped her. "Sit down."

"I can't sit," she said. "Your mother has a head wound."

He tugged her to a chair and handed her a bottle of water. "We should hear soon."

"She was there, on the floor. That man got inside somehow and attacked the wrong person."

Nathan knew all the facts. A small window just off the narrow backside of the wraparound porch. The man must have timed the patrol's walks and the cruiser's route, then he'd ran to the backside of the house and managed to get upstairs. His *mamm* hadn't reset the alarm after she'd closed the shop. And he'd been so distracted, he hadn't noticed.

All it took was taking the window out. The big piece of glass had been lifted right out of the pane and then the screen ripped. Easy to open the window latch and climb right in. A small person, the officers had said.

But someone strong enough to hit his mother over the head.

Adina stared at her hands, a habit he'd noticed when she was upset. "Nathan, I need to leave your home. I need them to see me leaving so we can set a trap."

"*Neh*," he replied. "This isn't one of your books."

"It might not be, but these things do happen in real life. People are used as bait or decoys all the time."

"You will not do that."

"I can do that," she replied. "It's my choice."

He'd hit a nerve with her need to be independent, but every nerve in his body wanted this over with so she could be safe. He had to consider his *mamm*, too. Her place of business and her home had been attacked enough.

"We'll all go somewhere else until this is settled," he said. "We can stay with friends for a few days."

"What about the quilt shop?"

"We'll shut it down. Maybe they'll stop if no one is here for them to torment."

He watched as Adina processed this idea. "Maybe that could work, but only if it looks like we're going our separate ways."

"You mean, you'd leave and head one direction and we'd go the other way only to meet back up."

"*Ja*. To throw them off."

He couldn't decide if she really wanted to throw these people off, or if she wanted to draw them out—in her direction.

"Let's see what the doctor says," he decided. "We might wind up staying here near Mamm for the time being."

Adina took in a breath. "You're right. We can't do anything until we know Ruth is all right. I'm so sorry."

He took her hand. "We'll get through this."

Adina glanced around at the people hurrying by them, the sound of calls going out over a loudspeaker, doors shutting, equipment and food trays rattling. "The world just keeps turning," she said. "But we're caught in some sort of limbo, waiting for things to shift, waiting to hear news of my sister. I don't know if I can keep doing this to you and Ruth."

"We told you we want to help," he reminded her.

But Nathan had to wonder if this siege would ever truly end. How far was he willing to go to protect the woman he was beginning to care about more than he'd ever dreamed?

"Your mother will be okay. She has a mild concussion, so she'll need to rest. We'll keep her overnight for observation, but she can sleep. We've cleared her to rest and that means rest. No phones, television, talking, visiting, etcetera."

"Can I just see her for a moment?" Nathan asked, relief bringing on a weariness he'd never known. "Just to wave to her?"

The doctor nodded. "Be quick."

Adina held back, but the doctor motioned. "She did ask for both of you."

They followed the doctor to the room they'd put Ruth in. She lay still on a stack of pillows, her head bandaged. Nathan had rarely seen his *mamm* without her white *kapp*, but right now he wasn't going on protocol or customs.

"Mamm."

"I'm okay, Nathan," Ruth said as he took her hand. "I have a hard head."

Adina stood at the foot of the bed. Ruth glanced at her. "I know what you're thinking, but this is not your fault. Evil is what caused all of this. *Gott* chose you to stop that evil,

Adina. Never forget that. Your bravery might have brought these ugly people out of hiding, and that will save many lives and probably people's income down the road. If this man was truly price-gouging and he has hurt your sister, the world needs to know that. I'm willing to do my part."

"I am, too," Nathan said, glancing from his *mamm* back to Adina. "We will find a way. We will."

Adina nodded, her head down, a tear staining her face. "I want you to rest, Ruth. We can't stay long, so you just rest."

Ruth lifted her chin. "I told the nice officer what happened. It was so quick, I didn't see anyone coming. I think she must have hidden behind my armoire."

"She?" Adina's head came up and her eyes widened. "The person who hit you was a woman?"

Ruth nodded. "I thought they told you."

Nathan pushed at his chin. "They only told me you'd given them a description and they needed to get on it. I was so upset I didn't ask for details. Are you sure?"

"Very sure," Ruth replied. "I smelled her perfume. Vanilla and jasmine."

Adina put a hand to her heart. "Blythe had some lotion that smelled of jasmine."

Before they could continue, the nurse came in. "Okay, our patient needs to get some sleep now. You can visit again in the morning."

Nathan kissed Ruth on the cheek and Adina took her hand and held it.

"Take care," Nathan said. Ruth nodded, her eyes already closing.

When they were back in the waiting room, he stopped Adina there in the hallway. "What if that was Blythe who attacked my *mamm*?"

Adina turned to him, her cheeks flushed with anger.

"Blythe wouldn't do that. She wouldn't hurt your mother. I know that for a fact."

"Do you really?" he asked, frustration taking a hold on his emotions. "You don't know what she might do if she's desperate enough. Maybe she doesn't want you here and it's been her all along? What if she's the one behind sending these men, Adina?"

"I don't believe that," she said, shaking her head, her arms crossed in defiance, denial coloring her eyes. "I won't believe that. Someone is playing cruel tricks on us. That's the only answer."

"We don't know where she is, or what she's doing but if I find out Blythe Meissner broke into my home and tried to harm my *mamm*, I will make sure she gets the punishment she deserves."

Adina's eyes shined bright with anger and tears. "Nathan, I know my sister has done some unkind things, but Blythe wouldn't do this. She is not the one who is after us. Her husband is angry about something, and he's taking it out on her and me for some reason. And I am sorry for that."

He held her gaze, saw the pain in her eyes. Yet he couldn't concede right now. Not tonight. "*Ja*, so am I. Very sorry."

He turned and stalked away before he said more things he'd regret later. Right now, he only wanted this to be over. His *mamm* was a *gut* woman who didn't deserve this. And while he would follow through on his promise to help Adina, he wished these people had left his sweet *mamm* out of this. It wasn't Adina's fault that they'd come after his *mamm*. But her arrival here had certainly stirred things up in a bad way.

Adina didn't know what to do, where to go. She took off down the hallway, going in a different direction from

Nathan. His harsh words echoed in her head, making her doubt everything.

What if that had been Blythe in Ruth's room? Could she have been looking for Adina and maybe she panicked? *Neh*, her sister wouldn't do that. Blythe didn't have a mean bone in her body.

Adina kept her head down as she walked, wishing she could hide out in one of the many rooms in this maze of a building.

After calming down, she turned around to find the waiting room again. But everything looked the same. The long hallway stretched before her with patient rooms on each side. And a bay of windows at the end of the hall.

She read the many signs on the walls that pointed here or there. But she couldn't tell if she *was* here or there already.

She spotted a sign to the nurses' station and hurried that way. Someone could get her back to the ER waiting room.

Then she saw him. The big man who'd been on the off-road vehicle at Blythe's beach house. And he was coming straight toward Adina.

She twisted around to run back the way she'd thought she'd come, but the hallway was like a crossroad—four different ways. Had she turned left here? Or should she go to the right?

It didn't matter now. The man was after her, his dark gaze narrowing in on Adina as he stomped toward her. She glanced around, hoping to find a nurse or doctor to help.

No one. All the patient rooms looked the same. Then she noticed a sign that said East ER Waiting Room. Rushing in that direction, she remembered seeing the same sign earlier.

But the footsteps kept coming, faster now. Adina pivoted to the right, trying to find a place to hide. Her backbone burned hot, her damp palms shook with fear and anger. A food tray rack with the remains of several dinners sat waiting to be taken away. She rushed toward the big metal rack then turned it on its wheels and rammed it toward the man following her, taking him by surprise. He hit the rack and went down, tripping over the mess she'd left. The noise of crashing lids flying off containers and utensils hitting the floor brought several people running.

Adina kept going, sprinting for her life while the man tried to get past the leftover food now all over the hallway.

She looked back as she reached another turn. The man got up and ran past the shocked people standing near the mess she'd left.

When Adina turned to get away, someone grabbed her and held her against the wall.

She pushed at the hands holding her shoulders, her breath burning against her throat.

"It's me," he said. "Adina, it's me."

Nathan.

She left out a sigh of relief, then she twisted out of his arms and stood back, her anger now as palpable as his had been earlier. "What are you doing?"

"Looking for you," he said on a breathless rush of air. "I'm so sorry, Adina." Then he tugged her back. "But right now, we need to run."

THIRTEEN

Even though he'd apologized and tried to hold her hand all the way back to the waiting area, Adina didn't speak to Nathan the rest of the night. They sat in the waiting room after she'd reported the man chasing her, both quiet, weary, aggravated and lost in their own thoughts.

Adina rested her head against the wall behind her chair and tried to sleep, her arms wrapped against her stomach to keep her warm. She had nowhere to go, nowhere to hide. Yet she would not go back to Nathan's house. Not if he believed Blythe was behind all of this. Taking a deep breath, she worked on how to find a way out of her dilemma, but visions of the day came back to fill her head with worry and fear.

The dead man in the water. Ruth lying on the floor bleeding. Then the man chasing her through the hospital. A man who'd slipped away before the whole building had gone into lockdown.

They'd searched everywhere, even brought in the K-9 dogs. But the trail ended at the back of the big laundry room on the other side of this huge complex.

Now reporters were buzzing about asking questions and the word was out that a man had chased an Amish woman through the hospital corridors.

Soon, everyone would know. Maybe that would help Blythe, at least. If people knew she was missing, or had seen her, they might step up and help.

Simms showed up around midnight with doughnuts and coffee.

"I think we need to find y'all a safe house," he said without preamble.

Then he glanced from Adina to Nathan. "You two fighting or something?"

"Or something," she retorted. "Nathan thinks it was Blythe who attacked his *mamm*."

Simms took that information in with a silent stare toward the wall. Then he focused on Nathan like a laser. "Why do you think it might have been her?"

"Jasmine," Adina said before Nathan could speak. "Ruth smelled jasmine-scented perfume."

"And Blythe wore this stuff?"

"She loved jasmines. Talked about how they grow here all over town." Adina glared at Nathan. "But that does not make her a criminal."

Nathan sat up in his chair. "I told you, I'm sorry. Look, I was frustrated and concerned about my mother. You're the one who pointed out that Blythe wore that scent."

Adina gripped the wooden arms on her chair. "So it's my fault now? I should have kept that to myself. I would have if I'd known you'd jump to the wrong conclusion. A lot of women wear floral perfumes and lotions."

Simms let this go on for a moment, then held up his hand. "Quiet."

They both stared at him, silent and brooding.

"Lots of women do wear pretty, floral-smelling perfumes and lotions. Why would your sister attack Nathan's *mamm*?"

"She wouldn't," Adina insisted, glaring at Nathan. "It's just more of the evil these people bring. They're trying to mess with me for some reason. Maybe because I'm her sister, and nothing else."

Nathan held his hands over his knees. "I speculated that Blythe could be behind all of this."

"Speculated?" Adina huffed a sigh. "You said it right out loud."

Simms grunted and let out his own sigh. "I'm guessing that theory didn't go over well."

"*Neh*, it did not," Nathan replied, his gaze on Adina. "I'm *dumm*."

Simms nodded. "Maybe a tad."

Adina stood and paced. "Simms, I'll be happy to go to a safe house. But not with Nathan. He's done enough to help me. This is my war and I'll fight it until the end. I don't expect anyone to protect me from here on out other than those who get paid to do so."

"I told you I'd stay with you through this," Nathan said, his words hard and loud. "And I mean that."

"And I just told you, you don't need to feel obligated."

Simms stood and stretched. "It's been a long day. Tempers are high and the anxiety level right here is off the charts."

He went to the window and scanned the parking lot below.

"Nathan, she needs to be in a safe house. I can find one and I can also put extra protection on you and Ruth." Glancing around, he lowered his voice. "If you keep arguing, you'll get kicked out of the hospital. Let me give you a ride somewhere."

"I'm staying here," Nathan said.

Adina went to Simms. "Can you take me to Diane Kemp's house? Ruth told me she lives about five blocks toward the water to the east. She has a daughter who knows Blythe. I think they'd be willing to take me in for a night. Then tomorrow I'll find other accommodations."

Simms shrugged. "If that's what you want. I'll have to put a patrol on their house, too."

"Just for now," Adina said. "Clara is next on my list to talk to. You could question her, too."

Simms gave Nathan a stare. "You good with this?"

"I'm not good with this. She shouldn't have to move somewhere else."

"Your *mamm* was attacked, Nathan. That's bad enough, but now you resent me because you think her attacker was my sister."

"So I don't have a choice?" he asked her.

"*Neh*, not anymore," she replied. "I'll be safe and you can take care of Ruth. I hope she will recover and I'm sorry this happened. But I'll find out who did this, with or without your help."

When they were in his car, Simms asked, "Are you sure you want to do this? Stay with your friend instead of finding a safe house?"

"I should be safe with Diane and her daughter," Adina replied. "Diane told me if I needed anything, to let her know."

Simms checked the light traffic and glanced into the rearview mirror. "What's the address?"

She named the street number Ruth had written down when she'd first arrived and Clara's name had come up. "Five blocks east from the quilt shop, the peach-colored cottage on the left near the main road."

"I reckon that'll work."

He touched something on his dashboard and a map came to life. "Got it."

Adina snuggled against her door, thinking how strange to be riding in a car with a stranger in a strange town. "Why did you leave?" she asked to cut the silence.

Simms didn't respond right away, his silhouette like black stone. "That's a long story so we'll save it for another time."

Adina accepted that, too tired and antsy to argue. She might not be able to go back to Campton Creek, but she for certain sure would stay Amish, and she'd like to live here in Pinecraft.

But then, she'd have to see Nathan all the time. Maybe she should just start over somewhere new where no one had an inkling of who she really was or that she had a sister who'd gone down the wrong path.

Simms pulled up to the curb in front of Diane Kemp's cottage and then scanned the street before coming around to open the door for Adina. "All clear."

She stood, her bones weary, and took in the small house. "This might be a bad idea. They've had no warning."

"I'll wait until you're safe inside," Simms replied.

She had no other choice, so Adina went up the steps and gently knocked on the door. Once, then twice.

A light flickered on and a young woman with a long blond braid falling against her robe opened the door. Adina saw Diane hurrying up the hallway behind the woman. "Can I help—"

The young woman stopped, a hand going to her heart. "Blythe?"

"*Neh*, I'm Adina. I'm assuming you're Clara. Your *mamm* told me if I ever needed anything to *kumm* here to her home. I'm sorry for the late hour, but I have no other place to go tonight. Just for tonight."

Diane reached the door and opened it wide. "Adina, has something else happened?"

Adina nodded.

"*Kumm* in," Diane said. Then she glanced at Simms. "Who are you?"

He showed her his badge. "Her bodyguard until morning. I'll just sit out here by the door. You ladies get her settled."

Clara gave Simms an appreciative glance. "Would you like some *kaffe* or lemonade?"

"I'm good," Simms replied, his dark blue eyes always scanning.

Adina gave him a thankful nod and then she was swept up into the world of Diane and Clara. Both women started talking at once but Diane's first question caused Adina to catch her breath.

"We don't mind you being here, Adina, but what happened to make you leave Ruth and Nathan?"

Nathan woke with a start, his neck aching from sleeping with his head twisted to the side. They'd moved him to an area closer to his mother's room. The small couch was comfortable, but he longed for his bed. He watched nurses and orderlies coming and going in the dawn light, a weariness washing over him like an ocean tide, taking his energy with it.

He missed Adina already. But he couldn't leave his *mamm* here alone. Simms would watch out for Adina and as soon as Nathan could get his *mamm* somewhere safe, he would go to Diane's house and apologize. He'd been wrong to accuse Blythe of attacking his mother. One of the officers told him they'd swept the room for fingerprints, and they'd know something soon.

Soon maybe they'd have DNA, soon maybe they'd have fingerprints, soon maybe this would all be over.

But would Adina forgive him?

Pondering that, he stood to stretch and saw Simms walking up the long hallway toward him with a two-coffee container and a small brown bag.

"You look rough," his friend said without fanfare. "I have coffee and freshly baked bagels from that Seaside Café place that just opened."

"Bagels?" Nathan shook his head. "You are more *Englisch* every day."

Simms gave him a deadpan stare. "You don't have to accept my generous gesture."

Nathan took the bag and pulled out the warm cinnamon and raisin bagel. "Cream cheese, too. *Denke*." After they sat down and had a couple of bites, he asked, "If you're here, who's watching Adina?"

Simms sank back against his chair and took a long sip of his coffee. "I've got someone on the Kemp house. Don't doubt."

"I have lots of doubts," Nathan admitted.

Simms chewed his bagel for a minute then said, "You and Adina, what's up with that?"

"You know what's up," Nathan retorted. "She's looking for Blythe and now she's got a target on her back. Blythe was always troubling, but Adina is a *gut* person."

"Yeah, I know all that," Simms said, his eyes constantly roaming. "I mean, come on, man. You two shoot sparks all over the place like dancing live wires."

Nathan blinked and took another swig of coffee. "I'm not clear on what you mean."

"I think you and Adina like each other, even though she's madder than a wet hen right now."

Nathan lost his appetite. He stood to stretch. "I need to go check on my *mamm*."

Simms stood, too. "Oh, I see. It's that way."

"*Ja*, it's that way," Nathan said, wishing Simms wasn't so observant. "Have you any updates?"

"I do," Simms said. "The DNA from the blood on the apron and that from Adina's fingernails matches two different men. The dead one and the one we're holding. So one can't talk and one's gonna need to start talking. But he probably won't since his friend went for that swim with the fishes. Still searching for off-road man." He took a bite of his bagel and added, "The dead one has a long record of doing nefarious deeds. And so does the one we're holding. Several warrants out on him as we both know. One happened to involve an aggravated assault felony, or we would have let him go by now. We have connected him to the Black Octopus Company. The tattoo is a dead giveaway, but we've got solid evidence that he's on Meissner's payroll. Now that the judge has denied bail, we can let Adina ID him in a lineup and that will be the final straw for him. So there is a ray of hope there."

Nathan stood still, a shred of relief fueling his heart. "Could we be getting somewhere finally?"

"We've been working toward that goal," Simms said. "I'm going to find Meissner."

"I want to be there when you do," Nathan said.

Simms gave him a hard stare. "Okay."

Simms sat back down and pulled out his phone while Nathan went to see his *mamm*. The door was partially open, so he peeked in. "Mamm?"

"Nathan, *kumm* in," she said. "I'm all better. You can take me home later today. Where's Adina?"

Nathan rubbed his neck. "She…ah…went to stay with Diane and her daughter—Carla, Clara?"

Ruth sat up more, her frown growing. "It's Clara and I'd

planned to warn her about that girl. She likes to party too much and she hangs out at the beach a lot. Why on earth did Adina go there in the middle of the night?"

Nathan couldn't look at his *mamm*.

"You angered her, didn't you? Because of me and what happened?"

"I made an assumption she didn't agree with."

"And what was that assumption?"

"When you said a woman attacked you, I suggested it might have been Blythe."

His mother let out a moan, causing him to finally lift his head. "*Mamm?*"

"We promised her, Nathan. Now she's scared and mercy knows what Clara's feeding into her tired brain. That girl likes to gossip and stir the pot. A lot."

"Well, maybe she'll know something about Blythe. This is getting too out of hand. You could have been seriously injured."

"I can't believe you said that to her. The poor girl is so frightened and…she cares about you."

Nathan nodded. "I feel bad about it, but I was worried about you. Adina is in a safe place. Simms has people watching the house and guarding our home."

"You need to go to her, tell her you're sorry."

"I need to take care of getting you somewhere safe, then I'll lock down the shop and the house. I got the best security system I could find and it can work if we learn to set it each night."

"I'm sorry I forgot," his *mamm* said. "I can go and stay with Ellen. She has locks all over her doors and windows and a high fence around her house."

"That sounds reasonable," he said, thinking of all he'd neglected lately. "I'll call the two clients I'm doing repair work with right now and tell them the truth—you had to come to the hospital after someone broke in our home."

"And then you go and talk to Adina. She might be safe at Diane's home, but you still need to make things right with her."

"I'll try," he said. "I feel horrible about what I said, but it's odd that a woman attacked you. Who else would be involved in this?"

"I don't know," his mother replied, "but I can't see it being Blythe. She could just knock and *kumm* in."

Nathan couldn't argue with that, but this problem nagged him, and made him think he was missing something. "How did you figure out it was a woman. I mean the perfume, you said. That's what got me in this mess. I mentioned the jasmine perfume and I put that with Blythe because Adina told me Blythe loved the scent."

"Well, that makes more sense, but this girl was taller than I remember Blythe being. And she had green eyes."

Nathan took that in. "And she was dressed in black?"

"*Ja*, black pants and a turtleneck and she wore a mask, but I saw her eyes up close when I turned up the propane lamp by my bed."

"I'll tell Simms what you've told me. He might want to talk to you himself."

"I'll be here until I'm released. You should go and then return after the midday meal. I'll be ready then."

Nathan patted her hand. "I love you, Mamm."

"I love you, *sohn*."

He left the room, made sure someone from the station was guarding her door and the hallway, then found Simms standing at a big window, staring out at the parking lot.

"Can you keep someone stationed at Mamm's door?"

Nathan asked. "I need to take care of some things before I see Adina."

"Sure," Simms said, giving him a quick smirk. "We'll get this over and done soon, Nathan. Because you need to let that girl know how you feel about her. Or you could lose her."

Nathan wondered if his friend spoke from personal experience. But he wasn't ready to admit anything to Simms about his feelings for Adina.

FOURTEEN

Last night, Adina had decided honesty was the best policy. So she'd answered Diane's question with as much honesty as possible.

"Ruth was attacked in her room so I needed to remove myself from her home and her place of business. But I had nowhere to go. Nathan stayed at the hospital and I asked one of the officers to bring me here. I still had your note in my backpack."

"You were smart to leave," Clara said, her eyes bright with curiosity. "We're so boring, no one ever bothers us." She shrugged. "Blythe and I always had *gut* times. She'd sneak away and we'd frolic, shop, go to the shore. But I am worried that I haven't seen her in a while now. I thought I saw her last week, but she didn't turn around when I called out to her."

Her *mamm* frowned at her then glanced at Adina. "Clara wants to be out there where all the fun is, but you need to stay out of the public eye, ain't so?"

"For now," Adina replied. "I'm so sorry to impose. I'll only stay tonight. Tomorrow, I'll figure something out." She gave Clara what she hoped was an earnest glance. "I'd really like to hear about my sister. If you're one of the last to have seen her, you might have a clue as to what was going on and why she had to sneak out for just about everything."

"I will try," Clara replied, her tone cool now. "I should have talked to you sooner, but I thought you'd find her safe and sound and then we'd all have a laugh and life would return to normal." She shrugged. "And I had several double shifts at the bakery."

"I understand," Adina replied. "I would like a normal life again."

"That could still happen," Diane said, but she didn't sound so sure. Adina had sensed they knew more than they were saying.

Now, Adina sat in their small front room with a cup of *kaffe*, while they cleaned the breakfast dishes away. She'd offered to help, but Clara suggested she should go up front where she could see the pretty palms and blooming oleander bushes. This den was more like a sunroom with rows of paned windows on all sides, a bright, sunny spot full of potted plants and knickknacks. It must have been a true porch once since what looked like the front door opened out into it.

Adina sighed and thought about everything that had brought her to this spot. She scanned the street, wondering who could be out there watching her. A patrol car sat on the curb near the corner of the yard. She sipped the warm, strong brew and nibbled on an oatmeal cookie, her mind spinning out like a top.

"What do I do now?" she whispered to the balmy wind.

Where did she go from here? Back home, or out on her own?

She wouldn't leave until she knew what had happened to her sister. But she also needed to talk to Clara.

So she got up to take her cup into the kitchen but stopped just inside the open doorway when she heard voices.

"I'm being careful," she heard Clara say. "I'm worried."

Adina didn't move, her heart hitting against her ribs, her pulse tapping beats she was sure they'd hear. Eavesdropping was wrong, but she held her breath to see what they were saying.

"You and I both know Blythe was a troublemaker and her husband is a dangerous man. She messed where she shouldn't have and now, Adina is doing the same."

"I have to talk to her at least. We can't turn her away."

Adina had enough. She walked into the kitchen and stared at the two shocked women huddled by the sink.

"Adina, did you enjoy the sunroom?" Clara asked, her tone shrill.

"I did," Adina said. "Now I'm going to gather my things and find a safe place to stay. But first, Clara, you need to be completely honest with me about my sister. Was she a troublemaker? Or was she in real trouble? I need to know what everyone around here is trying to hide from me."

Diane and Clara took her into the kitchen.

"We didn't want to hurt your feelings," Diane said. "But Blythe ran with some dangerous people." She shook her head. "And frankly, we were afraid to get involved."

"Her husband," Clara added, her pinched expression full of fear and dread. "He is the dangerous one and I believe he's harmed her. Blythe changed over the last few weeks when we were hanging out, but she wouldn't tell me what was wrong. She lost her luster."

"Do you think he killed her?" Adina asked, having said that for the first time. It took her a moment to breathe again.

"I don't know," Clara admitted. "But I wouldn't put it past him. He runs a tight organization based on what was once his *daed*'s propane business."

"He now sells other things, so we hear," Diane said. "I

stayed quiet because he's so dangerous. But now, things have escalated and my friend got hurt."

"Which is exactly why I need to know everything," Adina said. "I won't put both of you in danger by staying here but tell me everything you know so I can report this to the police. They need all the evidence they can gather."

"You can't tell them who you've talked to," Clara said, her hands gripped together, her fingers twisted like ribbons caught on a tree. "He'd come after all of us."

"I just need the truth," Adina said in a stern tone, weariness dragging her down. "I want this to be over. I want Blythe to be safe. If she's caused trouble, I'll find a way to make that right, too."

Clara shot her *mamm* a glance. Diane nodded.

"Why don't you and I go up to my room and we'll talk," Clara said. "You do need to know the truth."

Later that day, Nathan got his *mamm* settled with her friend Ellen. She'd been right about Ellen having good security. Her house was off the street a bit, hidden behind towering oaks and magnolias and clusters of palmetto palms.

"I told you her home is like a fortress," Mamm said as he pulled the golf cart up the shell-covered lane. "I'll be safe here. And she's invited Adina, too."

"I'm going to talk to her later," he said. "She was determined to seek out Clara, so I'm giving her time to cool down. I wish I'd never said that about Blythe."

"You have some resentment toward Blythe, but Adina is not like her sister. Remember that."

"I already know that," he admitted. "Now, let's get you in there and I'll let Ellen pamper you for a few days."

"I want you to stay somewhere else, too," Mamm said. "With Simms maybe?"

"I'll think about it," he said. "But I don't want to leave our property."

Ellen's house was neat and sturdy, and well protected with a yapping Chihuahua named Echo and heavy locks on the doors and windows.

"My husband worked at a farm supply store that sold fencing supplies and secure doors and windows," Ellen explained. "He believed in protecting me."

Nathan thanked her and left, with Mamm and Ellen in the bedroom across the hall from Ellen's, putting Mamm's stuff away. He'd checked the front and back doors and the small yard. It would take a lot of effort to climb the high fences or penetrate those double locks on the doors. And there was Echo to deal with. The dog had growled low at Nathan as he was leaving.

She'd be safe for now.

He got back on his golf cart and headed the back way toward the shop, being careful that no one had seen him getting his mother into the house.

He'd just turned the corner onto the street home, taking one of the wide walking trails, when he looked up to see a big motorcycle heading toward him. The driver wore all black, including a helmet. The roaring machine accelerated when it neared Nathan's cart.

Nathan halted and jumped off the cart at the last moment. He landed on the asphalt, his hands burning from where he'd slid across the rough sidewalk, and watched as the motorcycle crashed into his cart, ramming it enough to turn it over. The cart hit a tree trunk and folded into a crumpled mess.

While the motorcycle sped off without a scratch.

Nathan sat there on the ground and listened as the bike's engine died down. Then he took a deep breath and let it out. He was okay, but he'd burned his palms and hit his chin on the way down.

He ignored the pain of that and jumped up. He needed to make sure his *mamm* and Adina were both okay.

Because there didn't seem to be a place in Pinecraft that he could hide either of them from this ongoing danger.

Adina took in the pastel colors of Clara's room. Light pink warred with muted mint and turquoise in the quilt and the curtains. A deep padded chair and matching ottoman shined a bright creamy yellow in one corner.

"This is nice," she said, thinking Clara's *mamm* had gone overboard a bit. Or maybe Clara had done this on her own. But the room was cozy and comfortable.

"I'm glad you like it. You'll be sleeping in the other bed." Clara motioned to a twin-size mattress across from the bigger single bed. "She puts all of her guests in here, even if I don't like them."

Adina gave her a twisted smile and dropped the nightgown Clara had offered her on the blue chenille spread. Then she got right to the point. "Now tell me what you can about my sister."

"You don't waste time," Clara replied, her shrewd gaze moving over Adina. "Blythe and I met at a frolic just after she'd arrived here last year. We hit it off right away. We're close in age and had a lot in common. She loved to quilt, so we'd meet at the shop and then walk around. But sometimes, we knew one of his men was following us. We'd try to lose him, but he'd keep showing up. I think she got in trouble about that, because after a few attempts to find some privacy, she gave up. Then we'd meet in one of the cafés up the street and her guard would stay outside. No way out of that."

"So was her guard for her protection or to keep her from straying?"

"He did not want her to stray," Clara said. "That is for certain sure." Clara halted and then sighed. "I saw bruises on her arms."

"Bruises?" Adina tried to imagine that. "That Hayden put there?"

"I think so," Clara replied. "She grew more and more distant and afraid until one day, she didn't show up for our regular lunch and walk about town."

"Didn't you find that odd?" Adina asked. "Did you try to get in touch with her?"

Clara grimaced and stared out the window. "*Ja*, I was concerned. I left her phone messages and even mailed her notes. But nothing."

"And you just let that go?"

Clara stood and paced, her hands together over her apron. "*Neh*, I tried to speak to Hayden but he didn't like her having friends. And he especially didn't like me because I'm single. He implied I was a bad influence. I asked one of his guards if I could check on Blythe, and the man told me to get off their property. I had to call a cab to get me home."

"So you've been to the house on the bay?"

"*Ja*. But I always got a creepy feeling when I was there. Blythe put on a good front, but she seemed nervous and jittery, not as fun as she was when we were out together. We started meeting in the park just past their property."

"I know that park," Adina replied. "We were there yesterday and we saw where the park ended and Hayden's property began." She didn't mention the dead man in the water. "I can see how you'd feel disturbed being at her home. It was a strange place."

"And I believe strange things go on there," Clara replied. "Blythe wouldn't say, but she hinted at a lot of men coming and going. 'Deliveries,' Hayden called them."

"Why didn't you go to the police?" Adina had to ask that question. If they were that close, wouldn't a friend report another friend as missing?

Clara stopped pacing, her frown deepening against her high cheekbones. Brushing at a strand of blond hair, she shook her head. "Blythe got in moods and wouldn't speak to anyone for days. The last time we talked, I asked if she was happy and she got angry with me. Accused me of being jealous."

That sounded like an echo of Aenti's rants. But when Adina looked back, Blythe had often accused Adina of being jealous, too. Both her *aenti* and her sister had teased her about that.

"She did get that way at times," she finally admitted to Clara. "I'm sorry."

"It's okay," Clara replied. "I begin to see her patterns, her moods. But Adina, I think it's because he medicated her and then took away the medication as a punishment. He's not a nice man."

Adina wiped at her eyes. "I should have *kumm* to check on her sooner."

"Everyone thought she had the dream life, but looks can be deceiving," Clara replied. "Something to remember."

"Do you think he's dealing in drugs?" Adina asked, hoping she was wrong.

"I think he's dealing in anything that will bring him more power and money," Clara admitted. "And he forces people to pay him under the table for their propane needs, more than they should be paying but they need it for their homes and business. He threatens to cut them off if they don't pay."

Then she got quiet, her eyes gleaming with some unknown fear. "I just know he's not kind and if he is hiding Blythe away, we might not ever see her again."

Adina wondered if this woman had told her everything. She was about to ask when Diane knocked softly on the door.

"Ruth is staying with Ellen," she said. "She's better and she's settled in for a while. Nathan has closed the shop and put a Vacation sign up. Now, he's out front wanting to talk to you, Adina."

"I'm not sure I want to see him," Adina said. "We didn't part on *gut* terms."

"He needs to see you though," Diane replied. "He came in from the back alley, and he's been hurt."

Adina stood and dashed out the door, her sneakers hitting the wooden floors of the hallway. She made it to the front of the long narrow house and stopped at the open door to the sunroom.

"Nathan?"

He had his back to her but when he turned, she ran to him. He had a big bruise on his face and his hands were raw with scrapes and scratches. She rushed to him and took one of his hands, examining his wounds.

"What happened?"

"A motorcycle ran me off the road. I mean, off the walking trail in the alley. My golf cart got smashed. I jumped off but hit the ground hard." Dropping his hand, he said, "I'm okay. I just needed to check on you and Mamm."

"Is Ruth safe?"

He nodded. "Simms checked with the patrol watching Ellen's house. They are fine, thankfully. Mamm hasn't seen me yet and I told Simms not to tell her what happened. She'll be in a panic when she hears, so I'll need to be the one to tell her."

"Sit down." She guided him to a chair. "I'll bring you some water and I'll get your hands and face cleaned up."

She hurried to the kitchen and got what she needed after digging through cabinets. Diane and Clara came in and found her there.

"Is he okay?" Clara asked.

"He got hurt in a golf cart accident. I'm going to tend his wounds."

She hurried back out and put the supplies on the table beside the wicker chair where he sat. Then she gave him a glass of ice water. "Drink this and take the aspirin."

He took a long drink and put the glass down on the table. "I don't need aspirin. I just had to make sure you're okay."

"I'm here and I'm fine. Clara and I have been comparing notes. I think this goes deeper than I'd ever imagined."

"On that we can agree," he replied, that hint of anger still with him. "They want me out of the way so they can reach you."

"You don't have to keep doing this," she reminded him. "I know how you truly feel about things."

He stilled her hand and held it away from his bruised jaw, his gaze meeting hers with a flare of awareness. "I'm in it now, Adina. And not just to find justice. But because of you. I shouldn't have said what I did before. I only want you safe."

"I am safe here for now," she replied. "But I worry about you." She handed him two aspirins and then held the glass toward him.

Nathan took a sip, took the pills and set the glass back

down. Then he took her hands in his. "I won't let them do this. Whatever it takes."

"It might take more than you're willing to bear," she reminded him. "This is my fight."

"*Neh*, Adina," he said, his hand moving to touch her face. "It is our fight. Together. You need to accept that you can't get rid of me that easily. Not now. Not ever."

She held his hands, her fingers touching the raw-edged burns that only falling on jagged shells and rocks could cause.

"But you accused my sister."

His eyes filled with humility. "I was wrong," he said. "After our fight, I spoke with my *mamm* and she believes the person who attacked her was taller than Blythe and had green eyes. I didn't know that before I said what I said."

She stared up at him, her heart taking on a thousand needles. "After talking to Clara, I'm more confused than ever. I just want the truth."

He let her words soak in. "We won't give up, no matter what we find."

"What do we do now, Nathan? What can we do to bring this to an end?"

"We pray and we plan," he replied. Then he tugged her close and kissed her. "We'll find a way."

Adina sighed. And she thought she heard a couple of sighs from within the house, too. But she didn't look back to see if Diane and Clara were watching them. She only had eyes for the man in front of her right now. She had to forgive him in order to keep him safe. After that, she didn't know what might become of their feelings for each other.

FIFTEEN

Nathan had put on a good front with Adina, but he still suspected her sister could be up to no good. He didn't like thinking that way, but Blythe had always been self-centered and willing to do whatever it took to get her way. Had married life given her the things she'd dreamed about? Or was she playing some strange game by hiding from her husband?

If he found out she'd run away on purpose, after all she'd caused Adina and Mamm and him, he'd never forgive her. And that meant he could never be with Adina, because Adina would choose her sister over him.

He hurried to check on Mamm and Ellen again, making sure he wasn't being followed. He'd gotten a call from one of his top clients. The woman was impatient but her money spent the same as a kind person. He had to get some work done or he'd lose this major account that could lead to more work, but not if his *mamm* was in danger again.

Relief washed over him when he saw the plainclothes officer Simms had sent over strolling the block. Knowing someone was watching out for Adina helped, too. But when he went around the corner to the back entrance, using the key Ellen had given him, Nathan spotted a lone man strolling up the alleyway. A man who stood out like a pine tree in a thatch of palmetto palms. Nathan got inside the yard quickly and hid near the gate he'd just locked. When the man kept walking, he breathed a sigh of relief. Probably just someone taking a shortcut. People did walk the lanes and alleys through this neighborhood.

But his instincts told him that man would return, just like the rest of them. He'd lost his trust in human beings over these last few days.

Once he was inside, Mamm greeted him with a glance. "Twice in one day. You need to get to work, Nathan." Then she saw his face and gasped, her hands going to her mouth. "*Was der schinner is letz?*"

"I'll explain what is wrong," he said. "A motorcycle hit my cart. I jumped off before it happened, but we'll need a new golf cart."

"The same people?" Ellen asked as she rushed to look at his wounds, her round face filled with dread.

"I believe so. Don't worry, Simms and his team are on it and Adina is safe. Meanwhile, I'm determined to get on with my work before I lose all my clients." He took off his straw hat and ran a hand through his hair. "I've stalled this particular client enough."

"You're hurt," Mamm said. "Let me look at your injuries and then you can rest."

"I'm okay," he said, not wanting to explain he'd seen Adina. "I'm going home after I get this one job done," he said, giving his *mamm* a warning stare. "I wish I could stay here with you two, but I saw the officer out front. Sandra Perkins wants some landscaping done and I'm anxious to try my hand at that, and she's getting impatient. I miss farming at times, so landscaping can be added to my skills, I reckon."

He wanted to stay hopeful and positive, but his worries

about the future held him back. He'd just have to trust in *Gott* and know that *Gott*'s will always came to fruition one way or another.

Ellen brought him some iced tea while Mamm gave him a quick nod that she understood his concerns, but her gaze lingered on his swollen jaw. "I don't like that you must work, but you need your income same as me. I hate shutting down the shop."

"We're allowed to take time off," he reminded his mother. "But I'd rather it was for fun and rest and not this. The work will take my mind off of things, I suppose."

"That's smart, Nathan," Ellen said. "Those rich *Englisch* pay *gut* money to others who create gardens we could do with one hand tied behind our back."

"For certain sure," Mamm said, shaking her head. "Your garden is proof of that, Ellen."

"I do it all myself, but my nephews help if I bake them a pie."

"I'll help if that's the case," Nathan replied, trying to sound chipper. Then he checked the windows and made sure the front gate was secure. No one about, but they could return tonight. He worried for Adina sitting there in that little cottage on the corner, where all the world could pass by.

Ellen stared at him. "Someone has tended your wounds already?"

"*Ja*, Adina," he reluctantly admitted, a heat running up his neck.

"So you saw Adina?" Mamm asked, her keen gaze narrowing in on him when he turned around. She could always read his moods.

"I did. We've made our peace, sort of. I think she has doubts regarding her sister, but Adina is so pure and sweet she can't condemn Blythe. They are family after all."

"So you were careful with your words this time?" Mamm asked.

"Very careful. I don't want to accuse anyone who isn't guilty and yet, I just can't let this go."

She pointed her finger at him. "Just keep it to yourself and maybe mention it to Simms, but don't discuss this with Adina again. That girl has been through enough."

"She has indeed," Ellen called from the kitchen. "I just worry about Clara. She, too, could be a bad influence but if she has information, she might do the right thing and help you find Blythe."

Nathan's backbone went cold as a shiver slid down his spine. "Adina insisted on going there, and Diane welcomed her. She refuses to return to our place and right now, it's best she doesn't. We decided we all need to be separated, and she's decided to stay there for now. Simms wants to move her soon, so I'll be watching out for her. You can be sure of that."

He wouldn't tell his *mamm* that he was more of a target now than Adina. They wanted him out of the way to get to her. He had to stay away from her, but he also had to protect her.

"I have no doubt," Mamm replied. "*Gott* sent her to us for a reason, Nathan."

He shook his head. "Well, if *Gott* is trying to match me, He is making sure it's a perfect match. If Adina and I survive this—and I mean, truly survive—then we should be able to get through anything."

Ellen's dark eyes grew two sizes wider. "Are you declaring you want a match with her, Nathan?"

Nathan winced. Had he really said that out loud? Ellen loved to have the scoop on the gossip around here.

Mamm gave him a wry smile. "Well?"

"You two stay safe and don't go outside. I have work to do," he said, hightailing it out of that little cottage without another word.

But *ja*, he did want a match with Adina. He just didn't see any way to make that happen right now.

Even though she'd only worked there a day or so, Adina missed the quilt shop. She liked being with happy, wise women all day as compared to her bitter, mean *aenti*.

Right now, after seeing Nathan hurt, and knowing Ruth was still healing, Adina wondered if she shouldn't just go home and marry someone, anyone. But she shuddered at the thought of doing that. She had to love the person she would spend her life with.

Nathan came to mind.

She pushed thoughts of him away and, instead, focused on everything Clara had told her. Why hadn't the police questioned some of Blythe's friends anyway? Of course, Clara had been afraid to talk to the authorities. Maybe she would do so now.

Clara came back into the bedroom with lemonade and oatmeal cookies. "You need to eat."

"I had breakfast." Adina wasn't hungry. "I want to help out around here, so don't spoil me."

"I'm glad Mamm talked you into staying a few days. No one knows you're here and our back porch is screened in and private, so they can't find you."

"They have ways of finding me," Adina replied, shivers tickling at her arms. "I just don't want anyone else to get hurt on my account."

"You could just give up on finding Blythe," Clara said, her tone serious. "Let the experts take over."

"I could, but they don't always know how to find out

things the way we do—being Amish and understanding how complicated that can be. We aren't violent people."

"Some of us aren't," Clara agreed. "But those men like Hayden Meissner, they don't care about tenets of our faith or the disciplines we live by. They take what they want and they don't care who they ruin."

Adina searched Clara's face and saw a gleam of hatred in her green eyes. "You're not telling me everything, are you?"

Clara's vision cleared and she smiled. "I'm assuming too much. I don't like Hayden. I enjoyed being with Blythe. She was fun and she made me laugh. I miss her and I want to find the truth, same as you."

Adina sat there with her cookie in her hand, a strange feeling overcoming her. She really didn't know any of these people very well but she had to trust that they had her best interest at heart, and that they'd want Blythe to be safe whether they liked her or not.

Now, she couldn't be sure about Clara's revelations. Did all of those things she'd mention take place or was Clara just imagining things because she liked being in on the thrill of it all?

Nathan pulled up to the Perkins house and admired the symmetry of the baby blue two-story house that stood on high stilts made of sturdy concrete. The white shutters and matching trim shouted *beach house*. But the yard did need some work. The palm trees reached to the sky, but they needed trimming. The bottom fronds dipped, sloppy and brown, away from the fresh green sprouts. He'd need a big ladder to trim those. The place needed weeding, and some mulch would help.

He got out of the truck he'd borrowed from Tanner Dawson's

store. Tanner was now renting trucks for moving and hauling, but he'd told Nathan no charge.

"Hear you're going through a lot right now. We're all watching out for Meissner and his men. Now that the authorities are involved, maybe they can shut down his monopoly. He makes veiled threats to people who don't sign up for his propane instead of the less expensive brands. And so far, no one has been able to stop him. This should end that."

"If we can find him and get proof of his evildoings," Nathan had replied. "Adina is beside herself worrying about her sister."

"It is off that Blythe just disappeared. You're a *gut* friend to help Adina."

Now he wondered why he was even worried about work when his life was a mess. He'd fallen for a woman who'd only brought danger and destruction into his life, and yet if he had it to do over again, he'd still have saved her from what was about to happen that night.

He went up the white stairs of the Perkins house and knocked on the big white door. Sandra opened it wide, a smile on her pretty face.

"Nathan, so good to see you. Thank you for coming. I know you said you had some personal things going on. I hope that's all better now."

Nathan believed in honesty. "I'll explain all of that, but let's go over what you have in mind for me to do with your yard first."

"Great. After we walk the property, we'll have a glass of fresh lemonade and I made some brownies. My weakness," she said, grinning. "Robert loves them, too. So every now and then I splurge."

Nathan nodded. "That can't hurt."

They went over the acreage and worked out a plan for

how he'd go about overhauling the whole lot. The last hurricane had tossed everything around and killed a lot of her plants.

Once they'd finished and were on the upper deck with their lemonade and brownies, Sandra turned to him, her long blond hair lifting in the ocean breeze. The air was tinged with a mist but the sun shimmered on the water like crystals falling on an azure blanket.

"Tell me all about what's going on," she finally said. "I hear you and your mother are in some kind of danger, but why would Meissner suddenly decide to harass you?"

Nathan let out a sigh. "News travels fast," he said.

"My husband is a lawyer. He hears things," she replied with a lift of her hand. "I'm asking because I need you to know something. We were once neighbors with Mr. Meissner. He owns a lot of property around here and he's a dangerous con man. And if he's after you, Nathan, you are indeed in trouble."

SIXTEEN

Nathan went home with more information on Hayden Meissner than he'd ever wanted to know. Sandra Perkins had contacts that went above the police station. She found someone to look up the county records, and provide details hidden behind many facades.

"I'm sure the police and sheriff officers and everyone else have all tried to find his hidden agendas, but he's the kind of man who'd have offshore accounts and shell companies. And I don't mean seashells."

She'd taken Nathan through a maze of organizations and the "friend" she'd called managed to find out things no one else had discovered.

"My husband is a lawyer, remember. He has people—investigators who can go deep into the dark web, which is probably where Meissner found the BOC—Black Octopus Company. They like to prey on people for money, drugs, illegal weapons and, sometimes, illegal trafficking."

"You don't think Blythe became a part of that, do you?" he'd asked, fear for Adina mounting with every minute. "That he'd send her away?"

Sandra's dramatic blue eyes widened even more. "I can't say for sure, but you might need to consider that. Blythe isn't the first woman he's pledged to love. When we met him, he had a pretty dark-headed woman who was as meek as a kitten. They weren't married yet, but he said he planned to marry her soon. She'd come from Tennessee, I believe."

"What happened to her?"

"He said she'd left, and because she didn't want to conform, he'd let her go. I don't know what happened to that poor girl. I never saw her again and then we bought this house and moved. And not a moment too soon. I always got shivers when I was around him. My husband offered him legal advice now and then, but he didn't care for the man either." Sandra let out a sigh. "We've always loved having your Amish community here. You are all so kind and…well…fun to talk to and be with. And the food—oh, my. But Hayden Meissner pretended to be Amish in order to gain control."

Nathan could only nod. "I can't believe you know all this."

Sandra took a sip of lemonade. "The Lord provides, Nathan. You were trying to meet my demands and so despite your current problems, somehow you made it a point to come here today. I wanted to talk to you about all the rumors I'd been hearing. The Lord knows these things."

"You could be right on that," Nathan admitted. "Mamm always says there are no coincidences. Only *Gott*'s will."

"I love your mother," Sandra replied. "I have so many of her quilts decorating this house."

"*Denke*," Nathan said.

"Okay, then, let's get you some information you can use to find Adina's sister. No one needs to live this nightmare."

Now Nathan had the maps she'd printed out and he planned to talk to Simms before he did anything else. He didn't want to get Adina's hopes up and he had to be careful even trying to see her.

He went straight to the station and asked for Simms.

The desk sergeant paged his friend, then told him to have a seat. It didn't take long for Simms to show up, but he looked ragged and wore old clothes.

"Homeless man today?" Nathan asked, knowing Simms lived for working undercover.

"Something like that," Simms replied. "No rest for the weary." He yawned. "What do you have for me?"

Nathan pulled out the maps he'd printed at Sandra's house. "My client, Sandra Perkins, used to own a home next to Hayden Meissner, out on the bay. She doesn't like him. And she said he had several girlfriends coming and going all the time, and almost married one young *Englisch* girl. But things didn't work out and she left."

"Left?" Simms studied the maps. "Or disappeared?"

"More like disappeared," Nathan said. "No proof, however. The Perkins moved to the house they're in now in Siesta Key, but Sandra helped me check the county records and…some other records."

"Like shell companies and offshore accounts records?"

"Ja."

Simms tugged at the bright green beanie he'd been wearing and ruffled his shaggy hair. "We've checked a few county records, too. Hard to pin down just how much property this man owns. A lot of it is swampland that can be reworked to build on—as long as it meets all the permits for flood zones and hurricane fortification."

Nathan stared out at the traffic. "So someone could go missing on his property and probably never be found?"

"The swamp gives and the swamp takes away, bro."

"And that's what scares me," Nathan admitted. "I have a fear of that happening to Adina. I won't let that happen to Adina."

"*We* won't," Simms replied. "I can't promise that for Blythe Meissner, however. But I won't give up, Nathan. You know, I left the Amish because of this kind of corruption in my own community. In my own family."

Nathan wasn't surprised, but he was shocked Simms had told him that much. "I'm sorry you had to do that, but you seem to be where you're needed."

"I like to be needed, but I see things no man should ever see."

Nathan nodded at that. "What should I do with this new information, Simms?"

"Hold it. I'll check into the other property your friend found, and *neh*, I don't want to know how she or her people got this far. But this could be useful to catch Meissner if he's holding his wife somewhere isolated and hard to reach."

"Okay," Nathan said. "I'm going to make the rounds and check in by phone on Mamm and Adina. I'm not thrilled with her staying at Diane's house. I hear Diane's daughter, Clara, likes to party and that only reminds me of Blythe. Adina isn't like that." He shrugged. "She is a good person who has a big heart."

"You've got it bad, Nathan," Simms said as he walked him toward the lobby. "I'm going to help you save your girl."

"I appreciate that, and you need to know I'm going to do what I can to make that happen, with or without this place."

Simms did an eye roll. "Don't be foolish."

"I'll be careful, but Adina and I have unfinished business and I aim to get through this because, good or bad, she'll need someone when this is over."

"We'll see to that," Simms said, giving Nathan a fist bump.

Nathan left with a worried heart. An image of Adina

alone in a swamp shack, surrounded by predators and human evil stilled his heart. Was this how love began? With such worry and fear merged with such joy and longing? With this need to protect and love someone that hurt so much, breathing became too hard?

He closed his eyes and stood still at the corner.

Father, if You can give me the strength to protect Adina and Mamm, I promise I will love Adina and cherish her for the rest of my life.

Nathan had always been a strong man, but these past few days he'd finally matured to a determined man. A man with a quest.

That also made him a dangerous man.

Adina helped Diane and Clara fold the laundry. Outside, the sunshine beckoned and her thoughts turned to Nathan. She hadn't seen him in two days and when he called yesterday, he didn't give her any new information. Not knowing what was happening beyond these walls had her pacing, the angst of this situation making her more and more despondent with each hour.

Clara came into the washroom to help Adina put the towels and sheets away. "You're bored, ain't so?"

Adina shook her head. "Not bored, just concerned. I have so many people to worry about."

"Nathan being at the top of that list?" Clara asked, smiling. She'd been kind, but Adina was afraid to open up to her.

"I care about Nathan and Ruth," she admitted. "I knew them back home. Ruth and my *mamm* were close. But I never imagined I'd be here and caught up in their lives this way."

Clara grinned. "I think you and Nathan make a *gut* match. All the girls here have sure tried with him."

"Including you?" Adina asked, curiosity getting the better of her.

"*Neh*," Clara replied. "I've had my eyes set on someone else but I don't think he's even aware." She shrugged. "I have fun flirting. I know he'll come around one day."

Diane called out, "I'm going to the market. If you'd both like to go, we can disguise Adina with a big bonnet. Do you want a blue one, or maybe a mint green bonnet?"

They went back into the living room. "Is that wise? I mean for me to go to the market with you?"

"We don't want to leave you here alone," Clara pointed out. "But I don't want Mamm to venture out by herself." Was she regretting this already?

"Of course not," Adina said. "I'll take the mint green bonnet to match my dress."

"You'll look like a pretty tulip," Diane said with a smile. "And we'll let our officer out there know so he can stay close while we run our errands."

Soon, they were on their way, walking along at a leisurely pace. Adina did feel hidden underneath the huge bonnet and she kept her head down. If anyone asked, she was a cousin visiting for a few days.

Still, she worried. But Diane had informed the officer watching their house, so someone was aware. While the man looked doubtful, he nodded and got clearance over the phone.

Adina relaxed as she spotted him drive slowly by while they walked the few blocks. Maybe she'd be safe in the middle of the day in a crowded market. The fresh air wafted around her, light and fresh, a hint of salty water in its mist. The day was warm with bees buzzing and butterflies fluttering by. A perfectly normal day in a place that had many beautiful days.

They made it to Yoder's Amish Village in a few minutes. Adina grinned as she saw the fresh produce. Then she spotted the pies and decided she'd buy one to show her appreciation to Diane and Clara. She was making her choice when Clara came up beside her.

"The key lime is *gut*," her friend said. "And I love the coconut cream."

"They both sound wonderful," Adina said. "I'll buy the coconut cream. I'm thankful you are letting me stay with you."

Clara moved close. "I'd hoped I might spot her again."

"Who?" Adina asked as she paid the clerk.

"A woman who looked like Blythe. The week you got here, I saw her. I called out and she turned and left."

"You thought you saw Blythe here?" Adina asked as she glanced around. "Your *mamm* mentioned the park, but we never discussed it."

Clara shrugged and fidgeted with a bag of apples. "I wasn't sure, so I didn't want to get your hopes up. But yes, it was here and she looked like Blythe."

"Why would she run away from you?"

Clara lifted her chin. "Maybe she saw one of her keepers coming to fetch her home."

Adina stopped in her tracks. "So you've seen her before with the guards as you told me, and then you saw her alone, you think. You're a witness, Clara. The police need to hear this. I don't understand why you didn't go to them immediately when you spotted her."

"*Neh*," Clara said in a sharp tone. Then she sighed. "My *mamm* is so worried for me, she told me to stay quiet. Hayden didn't like me at all. He could come after me if I report anything."

"Then I shouldn't be in your home," Adina replied, her

mind whirling with a feeling of dread. "Do you have anything else to tell me? I won't report it for now, but I just need to know the truth."

Clara bobbed her head. "I'm trying to be honest, but we're all on edge. We'd better go before someone spots you."

They hurried to find Diane. Adina wished she'd stayed away from this bustling place. She glanced around and watched as Amish blended with tourists of all nationalities, children ran by with ice cream cones, and shoppers loaded their carts and bags with fresh vegetables, baked breads and jellies and jams in pretty jars. She stood watching, fascinated by so much life going on as usual. Then she turned and saw a man watching her. She didn't recognize him, but she pivoted and pretended to be looking at some fresh tomatoes. When she stopped, the man stopped, his gaze always aimed toward her. The man became intent on following her around the store.

She was about to warn Clara when she looked up and saw Nathan coming right toward her, his focused expression conveying the same apprehension she'd had all morning. His deep frown made him look every bit as dangerous as the man now following her.

She glanced back at the slender man dressed in casual clothes, carrying a beach towel. He spotted Nathan then rushed up and called out, "Adina?"

Adina tried to run but the man took her by the arm. Then he shoved something cold against her side. "I'll shoot him if you try to get away."

She panicked after she saw the gun, her gaze hitting on Nathan. She tried to give him a warning look but he kept walking toward them.

"Tell him to stop, or you'll both be sorry."

"Nathan, go back," she shouted. "Stop."

That brought attention to her situation. People turned to stare. Adina distracted him by dropping the pie against his leg.

"Don't try that trick again," the man growled as he jumped back and took in his surroundings. "I will kill you and him."

Nathan didn't stop. He just kept walking toward them with no fear. While her heart tried to pop out of her chest, terror pushing against her lungs.

Adina tugged away from the man again, trying to get between Nathan and him. "Nathan, please stop!"

SEVENTEEN

"Adina, *kumm* with me now," Nathan said, moving past Clara, who stood there stunned. "I need to get you out of here."

The man showed Nathan the gun he had under a beach towel. "I'm getting her out of here, right now."

Nathan stepped in front of the man, his fear for Adina hidden behind his anger for this man. "You won't shoot me or her, not here in this public place. We're surrounded by police."

Nathan took Adina's other arm. "Let her go now, or you'll regret you ever entered these doors."

The man glanced around and saw other shoppers stopping to watch. Some had their phones out, looking for a scoop to put on social media, Nathan figured. He had to ignore all of that. He had to draw Adina away from this man so the police could rush in to take him. The patrolman watching Adina had called it in, but with so many people around the police were standing down while they tried to take the shot.

Nathan would not wait. He'd die before he let this monster take her.

Nathan stood firm, one hand on Adina's arm, his feet braced apart. "You won't kill an innocent woman in front of all these people. *Let her go.*"

Next thing Nathan knew, the man had the gun aimed at Adina's heart. "I can't do that."

"Yes, you can," Simms said from behind him. "If you shoot her, I shoot you. Don't make me do that."

The whole place went still. Nathan had let Adina go, but he wasn't budging. He kept his eyes on her, only her.

Simms moved in, then more officers showed up, waving everyone out of the market. "You're surrounded," Simms told him. "If you have any decency left, you will let this woman live."

The man shook his head and finally lowered the gun. "This ain't over. We need to talk to her, give her information on her sister."

Adina gasped. "If that's why you're after me, all you had to do was let me know where she is. You would have killed me if I'd gone with you."

"That's not happening now," Nathan replied. He tugged Adina away and stood in front of her while Simms moved toward the man.

But it wasn't over. The man pivoted and tried to run. Nathan watched as he and Simms scuffled back and forth.

Then another officer called, "Get down on the floor now."

Simms wrestled the man to the floor and held him, then cuffed him. "You really want to get away from us."

He had the man up and moving. "It's not you I'm worried about," the perpetrator kept saying over and over. "You don't understand."

"I think we do," Simms replied as he rushed him out the door.

Adina stayed by Nathan but turned to give Clara one last glance as he guided her toward the open market doors. Then she paused. "Nathan, he could have shot you."

"I knew Simms was here with backup. Let me get you somewhere safe."

A shot rang out, causing people to scatter and run.

Nathan ducked down, his hand over Adina's head.

He tugged her out the door and around the corner where the officer who'd been watching Diane's house stood by his cruiser.

"How did you know?" she asked, her words barely a whisper.

"Your guard called it in and Simms alerted me."

They heard gunfire again, then shouting and a scuffle. People were pouring out of the building and running for cover.

A mother with a baby ran by, both crying, the mother covering her baby with a blanket. Nathan motioned her behind him. Adina comforted the woman and took the baby into her arms.

"You're safe now," she whispered, holding the mother close, so they could both cover the baby.

Soon it was all over. The market went silent. Nathan breathed deeply and turned to Adina. "Are you all right?"

She bobbed her head. "I hope no one else got hurt. Where are Clara and Diane?"

Nathan moved Adina to the patrol car while the officer guarding them checked on the woman and her baby, then they heard static over his radio.

"Suspect shot by a sniper," the officer shouted to Nathan. "You two get in the cruiser."

Nathan guided her inside and shut the door. The officer took the woman and her wailing infant to a police SUV. She looked shocked and frightened.

Adina strained to see the terrified woman. "She's all alone with that baby. I should go to them."

"*Neh*, the officers are watching her. Let's stay here where it's safe."

Adina looked over at him. "I'm sorry."

"Don't apologize. Clara knew better than to bring you out into public like that. I'm just thankful the patrol did his job and followed along. Then he called it in, which saved you and probably others."

"Diane suggested it," Adina replied. "But I made the final decision. I needed some air. I needed—"

She stopped. "I need this to be over."

"We all want that and we're getting closer by the day."

A knock on the window jolted both of them.

Simms leaned in the front window. "Another Black Octopus man. We almost made it to the cruiser. But someone from a building across the street shot him dead."

"He kept saying he had to do this," Nathan replied. "I wouldn't want to work for that organization."

"It's losing several members by working for Meissner," Simms pointed out.

"Is anyone else hurt?" Adina asked. "My friends?"

"They're safe."

Nathan pointed to the building. "There they are."

Clara and Diane clutched each other as they exited the building with several other customers being waved out by what looked like a SWAT team.

Adina fell back against the seat. "What do we do now? The whole community is in danger. I can't find Blythe and the longer I stay here now that people have footage of me being held by that man, the more danger I'm causing for everyone. People were already talking about the break-ins and Blythe becoming a missing person. He'll just keep moving her until he takes her away for good."

Simms gave Nathan a nod.

Nathan turned to her. "Simms had suggested we stay at his place. It's isolated and secure and near the water. Mamm can *kumm* with us."

"Do I have any other choices?" she asked. "If it won't put anyone else in danger, I'll go."

Simms walked off, giving them some privacy.

"This is the best choice for now, Adina. Clara means well, but she's young and impulsive. She might not know just how dangerous this is."

Adina let that sink in. "Nathan, I think Clara knows more than she's saying. She's been feeding me little chunks of information she should have already told the police. I think she's hiding things—maybe she even knows where Blythe is, but she's not talking out of fear. She's very afraid of Hayden and she says he doesn't like her."

"All the more reason to leave her to the experts and get you to a safe place." He didn't say it to Adina, but maybe Simms could watch the other woman's comings and goings. "Did you leave anything at her place?"

"*Neh*, she loaned me the dress I'm wearing. I had nothing with me when we went to the hospital."

"I'll find you some more clothes."

"And grab my backpack."

"I'll try, but if it means protecting you, we'll need to leave that behind. I'll buy you a new backpack."

Adina could only nod and agree for now, but the look in her pretty eyes told him everything. She had only one link to her sister, and now she might have to leave that behind, too.

She glanced out the window as sirens filled the air and crowds started gathering.

Clara came running toward the car. "Adina, are you all right?"

"I'm not safe here," she whispered. "I might not ever be safe again. I have to move to another house, Clara."

"Where?" Clara asked. "So I won't be worried."

"We can't say," Nathan replied. "It's for the best."

Clara looked surprised and then cleared her throat. "Of course. I understand."

Adina looked over at her friend. "*Denke* for your help. Someone will get my belongings later today."

Clara nodded, her eyes bright with apprehension and questions.

Her green eyes.

Nathan waved Clara away and tugged Adina into his arms. "I've got you, Adina. I've got you. I'll be with you and Mamm and I'll do my best to take care of you."

She laid her head on his shoulder, while Nathan stared at the woman hurrying away from the patrol car.

Just before dusk, Nathan and Adina slipped away to go to Simms's house. Nathan's *mamm* had refused to leave Ellen's house.

"I'm staying here with Ellen. We've been fine, we get fresh air twice a day and Simms said he'll put a female plainclothes officer in the house with us."

She'd stood holding Adina's hand, her gaze on Nathan. "You go and take care of Adina."

After Simms had promised Nathan he'd also put a female officer with them in his house, Nathan had agreed. He told Adina he wouldn't ruin her reputation on top of everything else going on.

"I think my reputation is beyond hope at this point," she'd replied. But she was thankful that he cared enough to consider that.

Now, exhausted and tired of these mounting threats, Adina

went ahead of Nathan up the three wide steps to Simms's meager little cottage. In the moonlight, it looked ethereal and intriguing. A little rectangular house with what looked like steel support beams lifting it off the packed dirt underneath. It held a small front porch with one old lounge chair decorating it and was hidden from the world by mushrooming palm trees and what Simms called sand dune foliage.

Adina stopped while Simms unlocked at least three different door bolts. "I hear the ocean," she said before breathing in the balmy air.

"It's right outside the porch on the other side," he replied. "I like being near the water."

A petite female officer walked in behind them. "I've always wondered about your cottage, Simms," she said, nodding as she dropped her go bag down. "Now I get to see it firsthand."

"Don't go spilling my secrets, Patsy," Simms replied. "I won't bake you any more of that bread you like so much."

"Oh, he makes the best bread," she said as she took in her surroundings with a keen scan. "Full of pure grains and sprouts and all the good stuff. Sometimes he throws in pecans or walnuts. You sit down with that and some apple butter and you've got a meal. One reason I'm happy about this assignment."

"I have two fresh loaves in the bread box," Simms said. He shrugged. "I like to cook."

Nathan glanced around. "Built strong. I'm guessing you had some Amish friends help with this."

"Here and there," Simms admitted. "But I did most of it myself. I still know the old ways of building something to last."

Patsy chuckled. "Okay, how's the layout here? I want to get acclimated with all the exits."

"Two small bedrooms," Simms said. "One on each side of this living room. A bath in the hallway to the left. Kitchen is here, with a pantry that has an outside door to the right. It mirrors the bathroom in size. They both have high windows, but you can squeeze through one if need be."

"Not if I keep eating your bread," she quipped.

Adina admired the other woman's laid-back attitude, wishing she could be so relaxed.

Nathan followed Simms as he gave the tour, with Patsy walking behind him with Adina.

"You two can take this room," Simms said. "It's kind of a guest room, only I rarely have guests."

Adina took in the twin beds and the two slipper chairs. "Someone wanted a bit of girlie stuff in here."

"My sister," Simms replied. "She visits now and then." He paused on that note for a beat. "The bath is next to this room. Nathan, you get my room. I'll be in and out, so I'll take the couch. Adina, stay in as much as you can. If you want to take a quick walk, make sure Nathan is with you. Patsy will be armed and with you at all times, too."

Patsy nodded. "I'll second that."

Adina liked Patsy from the start. She was smart, talkative and she held her own with the male police officers who were a lot taller than her. Simms had told them Patsy had four boys ranging from ten to twenty. She was like a little drill sergeant. Her hair stood in short sprouts of garnished blond and she had a tough, strong presence. Right now, she wore jeans and a T-shirt embossed with palm trees and flamingos with the caption: "Just another day in paradise."

"Okay, so we're clear?" Simms asked.

"Clear," Patsy said, rocking on her hot pink athletic shoes.

Nathan nodded. "Just watch out for my *mamm*."

"Always," Simms said. "That stunt today means they're getting desperate. If our man hadn't warned us, Adina might have been taken away, or worse. No more outings. You're still alive because they want you alive, understand? That could change, however. And if you feel the need to leave this property, you'd better have a very good reason. Don't make our jobs even harder, got it?"

Adina gave him a straight stare. "Got it."

After Nathan had given her the things Clara had sent in a plastic tote bag, she'd gone through her belongings and found a note from Clara. But she hadn't shared that with Nathan and Simms.

The note read: *I'm so sorry, Adina. We shouldn't have forced you to go out. If you need anything, let me know please. I'll be very careful from now on. I'm afraid he might know I'm helping you. If I see Blythe or hear from her, I'll get word to you somehow. Here is my number, in case you need something.*

Still getting used to Amish using phones, Adina had tucked the note away. She didn't have a phone, so she wasn't sure how Clara thought they could communicate. Right now, she wasn't too worried about that.

Right now, she wanted sweet rest, but she didn't think she'd sleep at all. Nathan was as tense as a bulldog and Simms was a mystery that would have to be explained one day. Patsy was the down-to-earth go-to person in this group, she decided. And Patsy did have her private phone with her. Adina wasn't going to use it unless it was an emergency but knowing that brought her comfort all the same.

Then she looked into Nathan's eyes and saw the heat of his gaze moving over her face. She should be safe here in this cottage by the sea. But her heart suffered its own kind of danger. The kind of danger that could break her heart and leave her lovesick and lonely.

She'd fallen for Nathan. How could she protect him if she'd never be free to do so? Free from this knife-blade pain that kept telling her Blythe was in serious trouble this time. Clara had come so close to telling her more, but now that couldn't happen unless Adina stole a phone. She wouldn't do that. These people were trying so hard to help her.

She walked to the big windows, careful to stay out of sight. The ocean crashed and receded over and over, the rhythm making her drowsy. Patsy discreetly went into their bedroom after they'd had sandwiches for supper.

Nathan walked up behind Adina and touched a hand to her shoulder. "How you doing?"

"I'm tired, but I do feel safe for now. This place is truly like a little paradise."

"If we can get past the evil that's been hovering over us."

"I'm beginning to think these people will never let up."

He tugged her close and put his hand over hers. "I'm here. I'm all in with you on this."

"But I've only brought you trouble."

He nodded, chuckled. "*Ja*, that's true, but the trouble is not of your making. These evil people brought trouble when they took Blythe away. Sooner or later, someone has to bring them down. I don't mind that if it keeps you safe."

They stood staring at the sunset off to the west while the night settled over the water and the moon sent glistening sparkles across the blue-black waves.

"It's so beautiful," she said, the warmth of his hand covering hers, giving her hope. "What happens when this is over?"

"We get to know each other properly," he said. "I think that might be a *gut* start."

"I'd like that," she admitted, smiling. Then she yawned. "Oh, pardon me."

He tugged her to the small leather couch. "You should get some rest. I'll keep watch until Simms gets back."

Patsy came out as if on cue and said, "Adina, if you're ready for bed, I'm all done in the bathroom. And I won't leave you alone after lights out."

"Neither will I," Nathan promised. "We'll get through this."

Patsy spun back around and went into the bedroom, knowing when to make an exit.

Adina got ready for sleep, her mind whirling with all the close calls they'd been through.

Nathan stopped her before she went to her bedroom.

"I do have one question."

"What's that?"

"Have you noticed Clara has green eyes?"

EIGHTEEN

Adina stared across at him. "*Ja*, I've noticed that." Then realization took over. "You can't be thinking she's the one who attacked your *mamm*. First you accuse Blythe and now Clara?"

"I'm not accusing anyone," he replied in a whisper. "I just happened to get a *gut* look at her today. She has vivid green eyes."

"A lot of women have green eyes. She's terrified of Hayden Meissner. She was shocked today. I can't believe she'd be part of this. She wants to help me."

"Or she wants information from you."

Adina stood and paced, wondering why he wanted to pin this on someone besides the man behind all of it. She whirled back toward him and stared at him. She was about to let him have a piece of her mind, but she stopped.

His expression held an earnest tension while his eyes held a solid resolve. "Adina?"

She tilted her head and let out a sigh. "I have concerns, Nathan. I told you I thought she could know more and now, when I think about it, she only just today mentioned she thought she'd seen Blythe at the market a while back, but earlier her mother had told me the park. Clara was vague about it, and she didn't even report it to the police. Why wouldn't she have told me or them that right away?"

Nathan led her back to the sofa. "She might be working for him. If she knew Blythe and he didn't like her being around or enticing his wife to go out with her, maybe he threatened her in some way. He could be manipulating her to serve his purposes. She might be a bit naive and think she's truly trying to help, or she could be a go-between to throw us off."

"She did seem excited to take me to the market. But Diane suggested it."

"What if Clara planted something in her *mamm*'s head to give her that idea?"

Adina thought about that. "Such as I was bored and wanted to get out of the house?"

"Did Clara say that?"

"She mentioned that I looked bored."

Nathan kept his gaze on her. "I have to look at every angle, every clue. Simms needs to know this."

"I don't want to accuse her if she was only trying to help."

"Better that than her luring you away like she did today. That man almost took you today. And she was standing right there to witness it."

A chill went up Adina's spine. "I don't know who to trust."

He pulled her close. "You trust me," he said, his breath warm on her neck. "You trust the people who know what they're doing." Then he lifted her chin with his finger. "And we must trust the Lord. Always."

She hugged him tight. "*Ja*, I need to remember that first and foremost."

Nathan smiled and kissed her. "His will. We have to stay strong for those who are weak, ain't so?"

"We do, but it's hard at times."

"Let's sit here and listen to the quiet," he suggested. "Listen to that vast body of water while we trust in *Gott* to see us through."

Adina did that. She sat wrapped in a plaid flannel blanket and curled up in Nathan's arms and drifted off to a peaceful sleep for the first time in weeks.

But that peace was soon shattered when they heard an explosion blasting through the night.

Nathan bolted up and lifted Adina into the air, then held her down again. Patsy came running out of the bedroom fully clothed and armed, her weapon drawn as she searched every corner.

"Get down behind the couch," she shouted, "and stay there."

Nathan quickly hurried Adina to the back of the couch, away from the sliding glass doors that faced the ocean. The smell of smoke permeated the air.

"Is the house on fire?" Adina asked, her voice husky, her words shaky.

Patsy moved from room to room like a stalking tiger, checking the windows and doors. "It's not the house. It's a small shed about fifteen yards away from the house. It's not there anymore, but what's left of it is burning. They're trying to distract us. I have to call Simms."

She moved back and forth, checking blinds and curtains. "Just stay there on the floor. If either of these doors burst open, I'll fire this Glock and you two run out the pantry door, and follow the shoreline to the west, got it?"

"Understood," Nathan replied. Adina crouched close to him, her eyes bright with apprehension. "Are you all right?" he asked.

"I'm fine. Scared, but okay. How did they find us so quickly?"

"Meissner's mole must know our every move."

"I hope Simms is okay."

"Simms knows how these things go. Let's just hope they won't torch this house."

They listened while Patsy called in the explosion, her voice taut but steady. Soon they heard sirens roaring toward them. Nathan prayed for all of them as he held Adina there. The weariness of running for his life and trying to keep everyone safe wore on him like a burning yoke. He wanted to go out there and tell these evil criminals to take him and let Adina go. But that would be foolish.

Patsy halted at the left window facing away from the water, then she spoke into the radio on her shoulder. "I see movement. I need that backup now!"

They heard a crash in the bedroom where Patsy had been sleeping. Where Adina had planned to sleep. Nathan was thankful she'd been sitting there with him on the couch.

"Go," she told Nathan and Adina. "Sneak around the corner of the house and stick to the trees along the shore, but do not come back, no matter what, you hear me?"

"Patsy," Adina called, "I can't let you do this."

"Nathan, get her out of here," Patsy said. "Now."

Nathan tugged Adina along, stopping at the other door to make sure no one was there. While he checked, Adina searched for a weapon and spotted a plastic spray can of bleach. She could put someone's eyes out with that.

Nathan looked through the cracked door, then leaned out. After he motioned to her, he took the spray bottle of bleach and nodded.

As they reached the corner, they heard footsteps running. Nathan pushed her back and waited, the spray bottle ready. As a figure rounded the corner of the house, Nathan stuck out his booted foot. The dark bulky figure tripped and went down. Nathan started spraying the person lying there in dark clothing. He aimed at the man's head first and centered the sprays of bleach right between his eyes. It only took seconds, but the man screamed in pain and writhed on the ground.

Nathan grabbed the weapon the man had dropped and then they were off and running into the darkness, merging with the shadows, their feet hitting wet sand, sea spray dampening their clothes as the chill of the night enclosed them. They'd made it about a quarter of a mile when they heard shots piercing through the night, and then another explosion.

Adina screamed and turned to see a fireball hissing through the night. "Nathan, Patsy was in there. She's in there and Simms might be, too."

Nathan held her with one hand while still holding the sleek black rifle in the other. "I know. I know. I pray they made it out."

The sirens had died down now, but the smell of fire and smoke wafting through the tropical breeze shifted the night into a sinister, flaming darkness. The ocean crashed and crested, but the hiss of fire sizzled through the night.

"We have to go back," she cried, torment in her words. "Nathan?"

"*Neh*, Patsy was doing her job. Remember, she said *no matter what*? We need to keep walking until we find a less isolated place. Let's go. We'll find Simms come daylight."

Adina pulled away and stared at the bright fire down the beach. "Simms has lost his home because of me." She sank down onto the sand. "How do I fight someone so evil and callous, someone who disregards human lives in such brutal ways?"

Nathan sat down next to her and held her hand, careful to keep the rifle pointed away. "Don't shut down, Adina. Don't give up."

"I'm not going to give up," she said, the anger of her words crashing like the water in front of them. "But I am going to find a way to end this once and for all."

Nathan didn't like the sound of that. "Don't do anything that could put you in danger," he said, holding tight to her hand. "Just don't."

She didn't respond. She stared straight ahead as the waves gushed up on the shore and receded, taking sand with them.

When they heard voices shouting not far from where they were, Nathan lifted her up. "Patsy is a trained officer. Simms is the best at his job. We can't go back."

Adina took one last glance at the fire then turned to him, her silence showing him her trauma.

"We must keep moving," Nathan said. "*Kumm.*"

She didn't speak but she slowly started moving toward the west, her head forward, her shoulders straight. If he could have seen into her eyes, Nathan knew he'd find a strong, calculated resolve there. A resolve that could lead her to even more danger.

After an hour or so, they saw lights up ahead and found a small shopping center. Nothing was open since it was the middle of the night. But they kept walking.

"If I can find a phone at an all-night gas station, I can call Simms," Nathan told her. "He'll know what's going on."

"Not if they got to him first," she replied, her tone weary and worn. "That's what they do. They torment people." She stopped and stared out into the sea. "They destroy lives and I'm beginning to think they did that to Blythe…and I might not ever find her alive."

"I can't promise you that," he replied. "But you need to focus on taking care of yourself. Even if you walked away right now and went back home, they would find you. We have to see this through."

She gave him a glance that showed she was close to breaking. "I want to fight this with every fiber of my being, but I'm so tired. I've never had such evil in my life. Blythe is the only family I have left."

Nathan turned her so she had to face him. "You came here with a purpose and you're a strong woman, Adina. You've done everything possible to get to the truth regarding your sister. If you hadn't arrived here to find her, this evil man would have gone on with his life and continued his illegal activities. *Gott* put you here for a reason. We have to finish what is started. Please, hang on for a little longer."

She nodded, gulped in a breath and wrapped her arms around his shoulders. "I'll be okay. I'll do what must be done."

He saw an open store. "Let's go call for help." He didn't question her, but he didn't like the knife-sharp resolve in her words.

Simms found them and picked them up in an unmarked car. He looked even more scruffy and weary, his hair tousled, his jeans old and full of holes, soot on his face. His expression was stoic, his face holding a stony mountain rock demeanor. When Nathan handed him the rifle he'd hidden in some bushes before he made the phone call— "For evidence"— Simms didn't even blink.

Adina and Nathan got in the back seat and sat low.

"Tell us what happened," Adina said once they were leaving the gas station.

Simms found a small park and pulled the car over. "My house is damaged, but not completely destroyed. The bombs were mostly distractions, from what we can piece together. They wanted to force you out."

"Well, they did," Nathan replied. "But we managed to get away. Someone tried to follow us, but we hid until the voices died down."

"I'm guessing that spray-bottle of bleach helped. One of the intruders had bright red whelps all over his face."

"We used the bleach on him," Nathan said. "That's how I got his gun."

Simms gave him a wry twist of a grin. "Whatever works, man."

"And Patsy?" Adina asked, her throat tight, tears burning at her eyes.

Simms sighed. "Patsy was shot. She's in the ICU in the hospital but her prognosis is good." He paused, then inhaled a breath. "She took out two men trying to get into the house."

"She saved us," Adina said.

"Yes." Simms cranked the car again. "This is all over the news. A hotshot reporter got the scoop from someone and now drawn images of Blythe, based on her description, are up on all the local stations. Of course, we don't have pictures of her, but someone was willing to talk. And videos from the market incident are all over social media, something we can't control."

Adina started crying softly. "I should have put up flyers when I got here but…"

"But you've been running for your life from the time you stepped off that bus," Nathan added. "Adina, stop blaming yourself. You are trying to do right by your sister. There is no blame in doing the right thing."

"He's correct," Simms said. "But I think Nathan will agree with me that this is all on Hayden Meissner. The man is ghosting everyone, claiming that he's out there searching when all he's doing is sending his henchmen to aggravate or kill everyone around you. He wants you alive, Adina, but he's trying to scare you to make that happen."

"And he's trying to kill everyone who has tried to help me."

"Tried, but he hasn't succeeded," Simms reminded her. "Patsy is a strong woman. We will pray for her to make it, got that?"

She nodded and wiped her eyes. "Got it. Now we need to decide when and how we can finally get to Hayden Meissner and force some answers out of him."

As the dawn brightened to a glorious gold shot with pink, Simms glanced back at them. "Nathan, your girl has spunk."

"Too much so," he replied, giving Adina a measured glance.

"I don't have spunk," she protested. "I'm angry, so angry I could scream. I need to make this right. I want to see my sister again. I'm praying that we locate Hayden Meissner and end this so we can all find some peace." Then she lowered her head. "And some justice."

NINETEEN

In the end, Nathan and Simms decided because they'd tried hiding them in isolation and with other people, and that had failed, they'd take Adina and Ruth back to the shop, but they'd beef up the security with several officers on guard. Word about the whole situation was finally out all over the community. While earlier rumors had flared, most knew the truth now—Blythe Meissner was missing and someone was after her sister, Adina. The Amish merchants in the area didn't take this lightly. They passed the word so everyone would be even more on the alert.

"After the market shooting, we've had lots of tips called in or brought in," Simms told them when an officer had escorted Ruth back to the shop. "None of the tips have panned out yet, but the more people know about this, the more we might hear."

"And now that someone leaked a lot of this to the press," Nathan added, "it's no secret you're being threatened and harassed, Adina. Meissner won't have too many places to hide now. People are stepping forward with stories of what he's done to them. He is not a good man."

Glad to hear some encouraging news, she still needed assurance. "Simms, do we have enough guards? I don't want Ruth or Nathan to get hurt again."

Simms's expression deepened, his dark blue eyes like two locked windows no one could penetrate. "Around-the-clock. Three officers on each shift. Everyone from the mayor to the beat cops are taking this seriously. You will be well guarded. Believe me when I say everyone on this block and the next and the next will be watching out for all of you."

"We appreciate the protection," Ruth said to Simms. "*Denke* for bringing me home. I love Ellen, but I missed the quietness of my home."

"You'll be well protected this time," Simms replied. "It's too hot here for intruders now."

Ruth looked confused. Simms explained. "Too many police officers and aware citizens for them to try and do anything reckless again."

"*Ach, vell,*" Ruth said, shaking her head. "*Ja,* I think that's a *gut* idea—that they do not do anything reckless. Sounds like you have this covered. Go into the washroom and clean up, Simms. And you'll stay for supper."

He frowned but didn't argue. He gave Nathan a nod and stalked to the back of the house.

While Nathan made the rounds and checked the office and all the doors, Adina helped Ruth prepare a quick chicken and rice casserole made with frozen vegetables.

"I'll need to go to the market soon, but Nathan said someone would bring us groceries," Ruth told Adina while they worked. "I'll never take my ordinary life for granted again."

"Neither will I," Adina replied. When she thought of all they'd done on her behalf, she knew Ruth and Nathan would always have a special place in her heart. "I only wish you didn't have to go through this."

Ruth spread chunks of chicken across the big pan. "Life

brings us surprises and you sure were one of them. I'm thankful you're here." Then she gave Adina a direct stare. "You're a brave woman, but you need to be confident and assured you are here for a reason. Your sister needed you and you came. The rest will work out how it must. We pray things will turn out in our favor, but if not then we accept *Gott*'s will. Blaming yourself over and over won't change that."

Adina couldn't imagine why Ruth would be thankful for being harassed and put in danger, or why she was being so positive and kind about this awful situation, but she knew not to argue with Nathan's *mamm*. Instead of constantly apologizing, she needed to take action in any way she could. But she didn't want to jeopardize anyone's life again. If she could find a hint of Blythe's whereabouts, she would go to her.

"Have you heard how Patsy is doing?" she asked Simms when he came out of the washroom all clean and looking strange in dark Amish pants and a light blue shirt.

He swiped a hand across his damp hair. "Holding her own. They operated to get the bullet out of her left shoulder. Another inch or two and she wouldn't be alive."

"Will you rebuild your damaged house?"

Simms gave her a long perusal. "Do you think I should?"

"It's your home," she said, surprised he'd ask her opinion. "I liked it and I so wanted to see the sunrise over the ocean."

"I'll rebuild," he finally said. "It was a good home, besides I can't let these criminals ruin what I love." He glanced around and then gazed back at her. "And neither should you."

Adina let that and what Ruth had told her sink in. She would fight this and she would do whatever it took to protect these people who had saved her. No matter what.

Nathan came back from checking the storefront, but if he noticed the shift in the mood of the room, he didn't mention it. "Alarms are on and guards are at the doors. Simms, could you fill Adina in on the DNA results?"

Simms nodded. "One of the men matched the blood on your apron, Adina. The one we found floating in the ocean. The man in jail is begging for a plea bargain. We told him we'd consider that if he tells us what he knows. He's desperate and scared." He took the glass of iced tea Ruth handed him. "We still need to match the scrapings we got from your fingernails. Might be one of the two who came calling last night."

Nathan gave Adina a reassuring glance. "You were smart to save that evidence. Four of Meissner's men are dead now, but we are learning more about their operation."

"Only nothing about my sister."

"Not yet," Simms told her. "Meissner will get desperate, too. Then we'll find a weak spot."

They sat down to eat, but a few minutes into the meal, Simms got a call. "What's up, Joiner?"

Adina listened while he nodded his head. He ended the call and turned to her. "Adina, you have a visitor."

"Who?" she asked, surprised.

"Your *aenti,* Rita," he said with a shrug.

Adina stood so quickly, she almost toppled her tea glass over. "My *aenti* is here?"

Simms nodded. "And demanding to be let inside. What do you want us to do? It could be a ploy to get to you."

"Have your officer describe the person at the door," Nathan suggested.

Simms spoke into the phoned, then repeated what Joiner said. "Amish, petite, gray hair, round face, plump and she has a mole over her right eye."

"That's my *aenti*." She looked at Nathan. "She's *kumm* to make me go home. I can't do that. I won't do that."

"Then you don't have to," he said. "We can refuse to let her in."

Ruth sat still then held up her hand. "I can handle Rita," she said. "She's exposed out there and it's too dangerous to visit with her up front. Adina, if you allow her in, I'll handle her, understand?"

"I don't understand any of this, but I knew she'd show up one day," Adina replied. "I'll see her and I'll deal with her. So *ja*, let her in and I'll try to get rid of her quickly."

But in her heart, Adina knew this new problem wouldn't be an easy one for any of them.

Adina waited in the sitting room by the kitchen, her palms moist with a sheen of perspiration, terrible thoughts running through her head like a fast-moving train. How had her *aenti* found her?

Aenti Rita marched in, her gray hair poking out from her *kapp* like old straw, her eyes beaded into a frown that made it hard to see her pupils, the scent of eucalyptus and lemon hovering around her.

She put her hands on her hips and stared at Adina like a mad bulldog. "Adina Maas, you will be the death of me. Do you know how worried I've been, how I've prayed you hadn't come to harm or worse, suffered a horrible death?"

"It's *gut* to see you, too, Aenti," Adina said. "I came down to check on Blythe and I'm going to stay here. I'm sorry. I should have left you a note, but I had to leave quickly."

Her *aenti* looked confused. "Oh, right. I'm supposed to say that's okay? You know I have ways of finding out about what you girls are up to. Seems Blythe has left her husband, which is a scandal all on its own. And now you're out here stirring up trouble to find her. If Hayden hadn't *kumm* by looking for you both, I'da never known what was going on. You most certainly will not stay here. You're coming home with me first thing tomorrow."

A hot fear flowed over Adina. "Hayden? So he really is searching for Blythe?"

"Of course he is. The man is beside himself with worry and he's been humiliated. He told me just two days ago that you'd come marching in, accusing him of horrible things. So I had to find you and end this, to save your sister's marriage and what's left of your chances of getting married."

"That's odd that he traveled to see you, since I couldn't locate him to confront him about my sister not being here. He's lying, Aenti."

Aenti bowed up and shook her head, her chin bobbing. "Shut up. You don't know what you're talking about."

Adina remembered her vow to be strong and make no apologies. "I do know. He has taken Blythe away and now he's after me. I believe she knows something really bad about him and he obviously thinks I do, too."

"That man is not bad. He's kind and loving and, well, he gave me a chunk of money for putting up with the two of you. Paid for my bus ticket here."

"I for certain sure believe that," Adina replied. "But up until now, he has been fooling everyone with his money and homes and status. He's not a *gut* man."

"Nonsense. You just resent Blythe. But Elman has waited long enough. You will return and marry him, and we will go before the brethren and you will confess and this will all be over."

Adina glanced toward the kitchen, wondering if the others were listening. "I'm not going back with you. I am going to find Blythe and I'm going to stay here and work in the quilt shop out front."

Rita's small eyes stretched apart. Her breathing grew rough and steady, a sure sign she was angry. "We'll see about that." She reached for Adina. "You get your things and let's get out of here. I'll find us a room near the bus station."

Nathan came walking out of the kitchen, his eyes holding a shining gleam of both anger and amusement. "So you're Aenti Rita? We've heard a lot about you."

"And who are you?" Aenti asked, her lips tight like dry prunes.

"I'm Nathan Kohr." He walked up to Adina and took her hand. "I'm the man Adina is going to marry."

"What?" Adina asked at about the same time her *aenti* asked.

Nathan prayed Adina would play along with him, but then in his heart he realized with a lightning jolt that he did want to marry her. But would she have him?

He looked over at her, hoping she'd understand. "We've talked about it, but we haven't made it official. Now that your *aenti* is here and so concerned about your reputation, I think it's time we let the world know. I want you to be my wife, Adina. Then you won't have to answer to anyone you don't feel comfortable with. I will love and honor you and protect you."

Adina's eyes flared with what might be considered a happy glow, but then she stepped back. "He's correct, Aenti. We have been discussing this. We've become very close, what with running for our lives and trying to survive. I was almost kidnapped at the bus station, and Nathan, who also grew up in Campton Creek but lives here now, saved me from those men. Since then some horrible people have been stalking us, shooting at us, threatening us and causing everyone in the neighborhood to be afraid. And now, because you felt the need to show up here, you're in danger, too. What am I to do? How can I plan our marriage with all this evil and chaos around me?"

Nathan had never been prouder of a person. He knew in his heart then that Adina was the right woman for him. He now understood why he'd been holding out on getting married. He'd been waiting for her, only he didn't know he was waiting on her.

Her *aenti*, who'd been so vocal before, turned her beady eyes on him like a crow about to peck. "Nathan Kohr? Are you Ruth's son?"

The kitchen door burst open and Ruth and Simms walked out. Simms tried to hide a grin. But Ruth looked like she was loaded for bear. "He is indeed my son. Hello, Rita. It's been a while since we've seen each other. Would you like some supper? Adina helped me make a chicken casserole and we were eating our meal when the kind officer who's protecting us and our property, let us know you were here. *Kumm* now. We'll sit and chat, get this straightened out. But before we do, you must understand something. Adina is going to stay here with us for as long as she wants. We have a wedding to plan if we can stay alive long enough. I'm sure Adina would like both you and Blythe to be a part of that. But we must pray that Blythe is safe and will be back with us soon."

Still reeling from Nathan's declaration, and her *aenti*'s face when he'd explained, Adina could barely put food into her mouth. Aenti sat solid and firm, and for once, she was so shocked she didn't speak for at least thirty minutes. She fidgeted and flittered, her actions like those of a nervous hen searching for corn. What was she up to now?

"*Denke* for the nourishment," Aenti finally said to Ruth. "I'm sorry I burst in all mad. It's been a long, confusing trip."

Then she glanced at Adina, her look as close to an apology as she had ever seen. "I had no idea," her *aenti* said in a low voice. "I just had no idea."

At least Nathan's ruse had cooled her engines for a while. Aenti seemed to believe his words, even if Adina didn't.

Simms sat in his chair all loose-boned and amused. Despite the tension of danger all around them, this had been a somewhat comical night. A night full of revelations and surprises.

Adina told herself Nathan had no intention of marrying her. He was only trying to protect her. Once this was over, he'd go back to being his stoic, standoffish self and she'd have to find somewhere else to live.

She couldn't eat, so she silently prayed for Blythe and asked *Gott* to resolve this in His way, His time, His will. She had nothing left to shield her. She had to let the Lord take over.

After a rather awkward meal with very little conversation, Simms and Nathan went up front. Ruth tugged Aenti over to the kitchen for *kaffe* and some strawberry pie, her gaze on Adina, her hand motioning Adina to go into the sitting room.

Adina could use some quiet, so she went in and sat silent in the small room, reliving Nathan's words in her head. How she wished that had been a true proposal. She loved him already. He'd been noble and kind, but he only meant it to put a shield around her, only as a last resort. She didn't want to be a man's last resort. No one ever had to know they wouldn't be married for real.

Then he came walking into the room, his smile soft, his eyes rimmed with fatigue. "What a night," he said as he sat down beside her, the warmth of having him near dispersing all her fears.

She couldn't look into his beautiful eyes. "*Ja*, for certain sure."

"Adina—"

She turned to face him when a horrible sound pierced the night, a rapid repetition of guns being fired and people screaming. Two men burst into the back door.

Nathan grabbed Adina, but it was too late. A man rushed to grab her, hitting Nathan hard with his fist. Nathan fell back to the floor and moaned.

The two men grabbed Adina and dragged her out the door. Pushing her forward, they forced her into a waiting vehicle. She screamed, kicked, cried out, seeing two of the police guards slumped over in the alley.

Behind her, she heard Nathan shouting, saw Nathan and Simms running behind the dark car, heard more gunfire.

And then the car zoomed through the night like a huge black bird of prey, taking its captured victim away.

The last thing Adina remembered as she was propelled into her worst nightmare, was Nathan calling her name.

TWENTY

Nathan sat holding an ice pack on his face. He'd have a shiner, but he didn't care about that. All he could think about was Adina's screams as those men took her away.

"I tried to go after her, Simms," he said again. "I tried."

Simms breathed anger as he paced back and forth, calling people, putting out bulletins and trying to do what he could.

"I caught part of their plates," he told Nathan now, "but honestly, they probably have fake plates to throw us off." Touching a hand to Nathan's shoulder, he said, "I'm sorry. I promised all of you that I'd protect you." He beat a palm against the wall. "Never saw that one coming."

"What happened?" Nathan asked. "Simms, they have her. What happened?"

Simms leaned in. Ruth and a shell-shocked Rita were in the kitchen, talking to two officers. "I'm beginning to think Meissner brought Aenti down here to flush us out, man."

Nathan jolted off his chair and stomped into the kitchen.

"Was it you?" he asked Rita, his fists tightening against his side. "Did he make you *kumm* here to distract us so he could get to Adina? What do you know?"

Simms grabbed him. "Cool down, brother."

"I won't," Nathan said, yanking Simms's hand away.

"She knows something." He turned back to Rita. "Tell us, because if those sisters both die, it will be on your heart, understand."

Rita burst into tears. "Hayden told me I had to *kumm*. He was so worried and then, when I arrived, that girl who picked me up made it sound like this was all in Adina's head. That Blythe had run away, just as Hayden said. I believed them. I knew they were going to take her and I wanted to tell it at supper after I realized Adina wouldn't run away from a marriage proposal, but I panicked."

"What girl?" Nathan asked, his gaze hitting Simms.

Simms leaned in. "What girl? Their lives depend on this."

"Clara," Rita said, wiping at her sobs. "She told me Adina had seemed erratic when she stayed with Clara and her *mamm*. That she'd wanted to find Blythe and when she did, they'd planned to run away together."

Nathan shook his head. "Adina wouldn't say that. She wanted to find her sister. She wanted to have a life here— with me."

While he didn't know that for sure, he wanted her to stay, for him, not just because she had nowhere else to go. He should have told her his true feelings.

Rita burst into tears again. "I'm so sorry. I tried to do right by them but I'm not *gut* at it. Hayden was very convincing and he promised me I could move in with him and Blythe once he found her and brought her back. I believed him."

Ruth patted Rita on the back. "A lot of people have been fooled by this man. Clara is in his clutches now, and she had been lied to also. Diane will be devastated when she hears the truth."

"We have to find Clara," Simms said. "I'll send someone to her house."

"That girl told me all kinds of things. Told me doing this would make Blythe come home and everything would be all right."

Nathan stood over Rita, pitying her now. "Everything is not all right. I'm going to find Adina, and I'm going to make sure justice is served. Then everything will be all right."

He turned to face Simms. "I'm going with you to find her, and do not tell me any differently."

Simms gave him a measured stare. "Let's go, then."

They started by going back over all the properties they knew Hayden Meissner owned around Sarasota. Since they'd been researching the maps, they narrowed it down to one piece of land near a swampy inlet off the big bay.

"Let's send out some scouts first," Simms told Nathan. "That way, we won't be wasting our time."

"I don't know if I can wait," Nathan said. "I know where this land is. I've seen the no-trespassing signs. It's not fit for building."

"But is it fit for hiding people, or dumping bodies into the swamp?"

He nodded at Simms's question. "*Ja*. This has to be the place."

They headed out, but Nathan shook with anger, his feelings like a million bees stinging him, his skin burning, his heart on fire, his mind racing. "We can't be late. We can't get there too late, Simms."

His friend listened and took off like a rocket toward the main road. "I'm on it."

Adina couldn't breathe. Every breath hurt. She'd been bullied and taunted and bruised and now they dragged her over wet land that smelled of decay and darkness, the shrill of wild animals echoing through the dense trees, the rustle of something slithering away making her shake with awareness.

This place was not a paradise. It smelled of evil and death and a spewing hatred that breathed its own life. And it would take hers.

They came to an old barn hidden behind a thicket of pines and scrub oaks, and she watched as one of the men unlocked the heavy doors.

"Where are you taking me?" she asked, her words moving on shivers of dread. "What's happening?"

The men didn't respond. They just shoved her inside and slammed the door. Adina stood trembling, her bruised arms wrapped against her stomach. She turned and hit at the door.

"Let me out of here."

Then she heard a weak cry, like a baby lamb. "Adina?"

She moved through the dark, a slant of moonlight guiding her path. "Who's there?"

"It's me, Blythe. Sister, are you really here, or am I dreaming again?"

"Blythe?" Adina moved across the big square barn, reaching out so she wouldn't fall. "Call out again so I can find you."

"I'm in the corner," Blythe said. "Near the window."

Adina made her way to where the one window showed a grayish-white path, the sliver of moonlight shining like a guiding beacon. "Blythe?"

"Sister?"

Then she felt a hand touch her skirt. "You came."

Adina fell down and pulled her sister into her arms. "I did. I came to find you, and now they have taken me, too."

Blythe pushed at her tangled hair, her body small and

bony now, her clothes dirty and tattered. "*Neh*, you need to run away. Go." Blythe tried to push at her, but her sister was too weak to do much.

"I'm not leaving you," Adina said. "I've been looking for you for days now. I won't leave you."

Blythe touched Adina's face, her own smile frail. "He's evil. He takes what he wants and has everyone believing he's a wonderful, giving man. He's not. I tried to send you the evidence." She leaned close and whispered. "In the backpack."

Then she passed out.

"Blythe? Blythe, wake up."

Blythe lay there, too weak to move.

Adina got up and tried to see out the window, but all she saw was a dense jungle of overgrowth and tall trees. The world had disappeared. She was all alone.

When she heard the door rattling, she said a silent prayer, accepting that she might not survive. She'd protect her sister. She didn't have any choice. Quickly, she searched for a weapon, but there was none to be found.

Then she heard footsteps approaching, light and slow. "Adina?"

Adina squinted into the darkness. "Who's there?"

"It's me," Clara said. "Your new friend."

"Clara." She didn't question it. She knew her *friend* had betrayed her. "Have you been working with him all along?"

"Of course I have. He told me when we got rid of Blythe, I'd be his wife. I know how to make him happy. All Blythe did was whine and complain and spend his money on quilts and flip-flops. She has no taste."

Adina wanted to slap the other woman, but she had to protect Blythe. "What is it you both want, Clara?"

The doors opened again and this time the footsteps were hard and had a cadence that moved with precision.

"At long last, the Maas sisters are reunited."

Hayden Meissner had finally shown up.

Nathan thought he'd be crawling out of his skin if they didn't get there soon. Simms had called in the SWAT team and told Nathan they'd be right behind the team.

Simms's phone rang when they were halfway there.

He grabbed it and spoke. "What?" Then he said, "Let me pull over."

"We can't do that," Nathan shouted. "Go."

Simms turned to him. "It's Clara. She wants to talk to you."

Nathan took the phone. "Clara, have you heard from Adina?"

"She's right here," the woman said, "but she needs you to do her a favor."

He glanced at Simms, a shot of dread roiling through him. "Let me talk to her, then."

"Nathan?"

"Adina, are you all right? Did you manage to get away?"

"Nathan, I've found Blythe, but we're both being held. They think I have something important, but I only have my *backpack* and a few clothes. I don't know what to do."

Nathan's heartbeat was near explosive. "Adina?"

"She's not available right now," came the smooth male voice, "but if you don't find my flash drive, neither of the Maas sisters will be alive by morning."

"I don't know what you're asking for, but don't hurt them. Let them go. I'll take their place."

"You don't have what I need, but it has to be inside your home. Go and search, alone. You have one hour and I know you're with your detective friend. I had to get his phone number to call you. But if I even suspect you're bringing him with you, they will suffer."

The connection ended. "He has both of them. He thinks Adina left something in our home—a flash drive."

"You spoke with her—proof of life?" Simms asked.

"*Ja,* Clara is there. She's with him, as in helping him. I feared that."

"Did Adina give you any kind of hints?"

"She just said all she had was her backpack."

They both looked at each other. Simms hit his hand on the steering wheel. "Someone must have hidden the flash drive in that backpack. Adina carried it everywhere, and she kept saying Blythe had sent it to her."

Simms whipped the car around while he called in a report on the radio. "We're on our way to search the house. We have about an hour. If we're not there by then, go in."

They got to the shop in record time. Simms had his siren blinking but not screaming. Nathan ran through the back doors.

"Mamm, where is Adina's backpack?"

His mother and Rita jumped up from where they'd been waiting in the sitting room.

"There where she left it," Mamm said. "On the hall tree at the stairs."

Nathan saw the colorful butterflies, and then he grabbed the backpack and emptied it of her clothes and some books. "We've located them. Meissner has both Blythe and Adina. And, Mamm, Clara is there with him."

"Oh, my," Mamm said, looking at Rita. "It's true, then."

Rita started crying all over again. "My poor girls. I've done them wrong, Ruth. So wrong."

"You told us the truth, Rita. That might just save them."

Nathan turned toward the door. "I have to go. We don't have much time."

"Be safe," Mamm called out. "We are in prayer."

Nathan thought prayer would be the only thing that could save them now.

He was back in the car in under five minutes. They had a fifteen-minute drive if the traffic was heavy. Simms turned on the sirens to get them through the worst of it, and once they were on the less-traveled side road headed to the location, he turned the siren off. All the while talking to the radio.

But after parking some distance away and trekking through vines and weeds and dense clusters of palmetto palms, Nathan felt as if they'd been running a marathon.

They arrived, sweating and bug bitten, with two minutes to spare.

Simms stopped Nathan. "You'll need to go in alone, you know?"

"I have to, or he'll hurt them."

"Okay, you get in there and I'll have my team lined up. Listen to me, Nathan. Don't try to take him on your own. We have snipers for that."

Nathan wasn't listening. He had to get in there and save Adina. But he nodded. "Let me go."

TWENTY-ONE

Adina held Blythe close while Clara paced in front of them. Meissner stayed near the doors with his henchmen.

"Why are you doing this, Clara?" Adina asked. "Blythe was your friend. I thought we were friends."

"I got close to Blythe because I wanted to be close to Hayden. I felt something for him. He knew what I wanted out of life and I could see he wanted me."

Adina lowered her voice. "He's done this with several young girls, you know. He loves them and they disappear."

"I don't believe you."

"Then take a *gut* look at my sister. Does she look smug or happy now?"

Clara stumbled in her pacing. "That's because she didn't obey her husband. I will do anything to make Hayden happy."

"Even give up your soul?" Adina asked, stalling for time. She'd felt something against the wall and realized it must be an old piece of rebar, the kind of wiry bars she'd seen on construction sites. It could do damage.

"I won't be giving up anything," Clara hissed. "I'll be such a great wife, I'll be rewarded. Hayden has promised me a *gut* life."

"He promised Blythe that, too," Adina said, her hand

gripping the grimy old bar she'd found. "And look at her. Take a close look at what you've done to my sister."

Meissner stalked toward them. Adina saw his craggy face in the moonlight shadows. His eyes were an eerie black, his hair long and stringy. He looked like pure evil. "Stop talking. I can't hear myself think."

"They are taunting me," Clara said, her hand patting her hair. She grabbed his arm. "They don't know how much we love each other."

Meissner didn't even crack a smile.

"He'll kill Blythe in order to marry you," Adina said. "You know that, Clara. Are you willing to let that happen?"

"How else can I be his wife?" Clara asked, anger flaring in her eyes. "We tried to scare you away and you just kept coming. Now you'll both be out of the way for good."

Adina didn't say anything. She didn't plan to die. She'd thought she would, but now she felt a new energy busting through her fears. Nathan was on his way. They'd find a way out of this, together.

When the two henchmen heard a tap on the big doors, they opened them. Meissner shoved Clara away and hurried to the front of the building.

"Nathan Kohr," Meissner said, welcoming him as if they were at a picnic, "you only had a minute left."

"I'm here now," Nathan replied, a trace of dawn shining on his face. His profile was a rock wall of simmering anger.

Adina hoped he could see her. She blinked back tears and watched and waited for the right moment to help him.

"I have the only thing I could find of Adina's," Nathan said as he scanned the semi-dark barn. "Her backpack."

Blythe moaned, but Adina hushed her. "It will be all right."

"Adina?" Nathan called out. "Are you here?"

"I'm here," she said, her voice hoarse. "Blythe is with me, but she's very ill."

"She wouldn't eat," Clara blurted out. "So I stopped feeding her."

Adina had never felt hate before, but now it poured over her like a hot liquid. She held steady and ignored Clara's taunts. She would survive this, and somehow, she'd have to find a way to forgive these people.

Nathan moved forward, and the guards pushed him back. But he didn't back down. "I gave you the backpack, now let them go."

"You've all wasted my time for almost two weeks," Meissner said on a snarl. "A backpack does me no good."

"It has hidden pockets," Nathan replied. "I didn't check since I was in a hurry, but maybe you should."

Meissner took the backpack and handed it to one of his men. "Search it. If you don't find that flash drive, they'll all die."

Adina could just make out Nathan's frame in the coming dawn. She watched and when Meissner moved to the side with one of his men, she found her opportunity.

Clara took that time to lean over them, her smirk full of hatred and anger. "Nice knowing you, girls."

"Nice knowing you, too," Adina said. Then she swung the piece of rebar as hard as she could and hit Clara square on the face.

Clara let out a scream and held her hand to her face. Nathan whirled to grab the guard's gun, then tripped the man with his foot.

Meissner and the man with him had just found something in the backpack, and distracted, missed the whole thing until it was too late. They both whirled at all the noise.

The doors banged open and the barn became full of men

in heavy black vests and helmets. Meissner cursed and tried to run, but Nathan tagged him and held him against the wall.

"I don't think so."

Adina grabbed Blythe up, forcing her to stand while Clara screamed and ran in circles, searching for a way out. Adina watched as Nathan lifted his fist, ready to finish off Hayden Meissner.

But Simms pulled Nathan back. "We'll take over now, brother. Your work here is finished. Go take care of your girl."

Nathan turned and ran to Adina. "Are you all right?" he asked as she tried to help Blythe while the SWAT team surrounded them.

"I'm fine." Adina shifted her sister's weight. "But Blythe is very ill."

He swept Blythe up into his arms, and nudged Adina by his side. "Let's get her out of here."

Sirens whirled red through the dawn, and the countryside swarmed with law enforcement people.

A few minutes later, Adina stood with Nathan and watched an ambulance take her sister away. "I have to go be with her."

Simms walked up to them. "It's over. We have the flash drive. Blythe found it somehow and discovered the truth when she opened it, then she sewed it into the seam so no one would notice and mailed it to Adina. She managed to tell us that much. She was going to share all this with Adina when she arrived, but never got that chance. Clara told Meissner she thought Blythe had found something damaging, and that she planned to leave him. She helped hide her away and well…you know the rest. I'll get y'all to the hospital, but we'll need statements later."

Nathan took Adina by the hand and they got into the back of a patrol car to go and be with Blythe. Pulling her close, he kissed her cheek. "It's really over, Adina."

She snuggled against him, closed her eyes and thanked *Gott* for Nathan Kohr.

A few days later, after they brought Blythe home from the hospital and had her tucked safely on a cot in Adina's room, Nathan grabbed Adina by the hand.

"I have a surprise for you," he said, tugging her along. "Don't worry, Mamm is with Blythe."

She nodded and followed him out onto the front porch. She and her sister had a long talk when Blythe was recovering. They planned to stay here.

I want to be alone and rethink my life, Blythe had told her. *I want a simple life. I don't want to be married and I can't be married. I might be his wife in name only, but Hayden can't control me anymore. No man will.*

Adina felt sad for her sister, but Blythe seemed content for now. Her sister had changed, but she was still afraid and probably would always be afraid of men.

"Where are we going?" Adina asked Nathan now, trying to find something positive to think about.

"We're taking a bus to Siesta Key," he said. Then he lifted a basket out of one of the rocking chairs. "We'll have a picnic by the ocean."

Adina loved that idea, but she was still a bit shell-shocked. "I'm not sure—"

"It will be all right. Meissner is locked up. You've identified the man they were holding and Meissner's whole organization has been seized. They are all going to jail."

"And Clara?"

"She'll go to trial and if found guilty, she'll be in jail for a long, long time. Diane is moving to a relative's home in the Panhandle but plans to come and go during the trial."

Adina relaxed. She'd visited Clara in jail, but Clara wasn't ready to confess or apologize. "We could have had a great life," she'd told Adina. "But you ruined all of that."

Adina had looked her in the eye and said, "I forgive you." Then she'd left, the glare of Clara's hatred burning her as she walked away.

"Do you want to go?" Nathan asked, bringing her back to the here and now.

"I do," she replied. She wouldn't live in fear. She'd grown stronger through this ordeal and she'd never again think she had to apologize for the things she couldn't control. *Gott* was in control and that was all she needed to know.

Except, she wished *Gott* would show her the path she needed to be on. With the man she loved.

They walked along the street, greeting neighbors and enjoying the warm ocean breezes. Then they took a bus over the bridge to the bay and got off at a big park.

"Nathan," she said after they'd found a picnic table and spread the chicken salad sandwiches and chips out on their napkins and nibbled their food, "why are we here?"

"You don't know why?" he asked as he took her hand and guided her down to the sandy beach.

"Is this the part where you tell me you're glad we got through this, but now it's time for me to move on?"

He shook his head. "*Neh*, Adina, this is the part where I tell you I love you and I ask you to marry me. And this time, I mean it. I think I always meant it."

Adina's eyes watered as she gazed up at him. "So this would be the third time you've offered to marry me?"

"*Neh*, this will be the first time I ask you to marry me."

She gasped and stared up at him. "Do you mean that?"

"I do. I want to marry you and take care of you and have children with you and buy you a house near Mamm's so you can walk to work. And don't worry about Blythe. Your *aenti* is considering staying here and she has offered Blythe a place to live."

Adina couldn't believe this was real. "Aenti has for certain sure changed. And so have I."

"Is that a yes, then?"

"I didn't think you had it in you," she admitted.

"Neither did I," he replied. "Will you just give me an answer, please?"

"The answer is yes. *Ja*, I will marry you. I love you, Nathan."

"I love you, too," he replied.

Then they smiled and hugged and ran along the shore, the waves chasing their joy with a fresh mist that had both of them laughing, the echo of their happiness lifting up to the puffy white clouds like a bird taking flight.

Adina kissed him and then she closed her eyes and held her head up to the sunshine, her heart at peace.

At last.

* * * * *

Dear Reader,

I had a lot of fun writing an Amish suspense set in Pinecraft, Florida. It was a tough book to write because it's a new setting. My first Pinecraft story, *Pinecraft Refuge*, was a favorite with readers. While this one is set in the same place, it's a stand-alone book about a young Amish woman who only wants to find her wayward sister. Adina is shy and quiet but when a friend from her past comes to her rescue, her strengths begin to emerge. Nathan is a truly good man who has shied away from love. But together, they not only help to take down the bad guy. They also fall in love. I hope you enjoyed this story of two very different people being forced together in paradise.

I also hope you know that no matter where you live, or what kind of view you have out the window, and no matter what you're going through, you can find peace in your heart because God loves you.

Until next time, may the angels watch over you. Always.
Lenora Worth